short
and scary

Edited by Karen Tayleur

short
and scary

a whole lot of creepy stories
and other chilling stuff

Edited by Karen Tayleur

black dog

First published in 2010 by
black dog books
15 Gertrude Street
Fitzroy Vic 3065
Australia
+61 3 9419 9406
+61 3 9419 1214 (fax)
dog@bdb.com.au
www.bdb.com.au

Australian Government

This project has been assisted by the Australian Government through the Australia Council, its arts funding and advisory body.

10 9 8 7 6 5 4 3 2

10 11 12 13

Contents

Introduction
Karen Tayleur

I LOVE being scared. The heart-stopping, skin-crawling, jumping three metres in the air kind of scared, when you know that really everything is going to be all right but just for that split second your body thinks it might not be.

The scariest thing that happened to me as a kid was that my sister used to hide under my bed at night. Then, as I was getting into bed, she would grab one of my ankles and I'd scream until she let go. The worst thing was she didn't do it every night, so I'd forget that she might be there and then she would scare me again. It got to the stage where I would jump into bed from at least an arm's length away, just in case she was there. There are still moments now when I expect her hand to snake out from beneath my bed to grab at me.

I love scary stories. The best scary stories are those told late on a dark night by the light of a torch when you're hanging out with a bunch of your friends. Turn the torch off and it's even scarier.

So when black dog books asked me to edit their *short and scary* anthology, I thought about all the short things I was scared of. (Well, technically some of them are small, but I guess they are short as well.)

The list went something like this:

- earwigs (because an adult once told me that they crawl into your ear at night and eat your brains. Of course, this isn't true…)
- black shiny beetles (I think it's the way they scuttle across a floor)
- centipedes (too many feet, just imagine one crawling over you)
- two-year-olds with chocolate ice-cream-covered hands who want to give me a hug
- people with short tempers
- short films about scary monsters
- scary films about short monsters.

You will not find anything from my list in the *short and scary* anthology, except maybe some monsters with short tempers. But you will find many other scary things. In fact, it was interesting to see the things that authors and illustrators found scary. Inside this book you will find:

- things that go bump in the night
- modern technology takeovers
- monsters running amok
- nature taking revenge.

There are even scary fairy stories.

So you see, there is something for everyone.

Inside these pages you will discover new authors and illustrators as well as some old favourites who are DYING to scare you. The best thing about this book is that you can read it from cover to cover or just dip into it randomly.

The profits from the sale of this book will be donated to youth mentoring programs. We would like to thank our contributors who have donated their time and talent to making this possible.

Mega-walk

Carole Wilkinson

'**WE MAY** as well give up,' said Renata. 'Thanks to you, the others are way ahead.'

Jake was undoing his shoelace. Renata sighed. He'd lost the compass, left the map at the last information post, now he had a stone in his shoe. And he had no fashion sense. Renata couldn't believe Miss Fenton had paired her with Jake.

'It's only a bushcraft survival activity,' Jake said. 'Who cares?'

'I do. I like to win.'

'If we take a short cut through the forest we can beat the others,' Jake suggested.

'That's cheating. And anyway, the first rule of bushwalking is *Never Leave the Path*.'

Jake ignored Renata and plunged into the forest.

'Now we're really lost,' said Renata half-an-hour later.

'No, we're not. I can hear voices.' Jake ploughed off through the trees again.

'I can hear something too,' she said, 'but it's not voices. It sounds more like…' They rounded a rocky outcrop and found themselves at the base of a thundering waterfall. '…water.'

Renata tried to picture the lost map. She couldn't remember seeing a waterfall marked on it.

'The creek's too deep to cross,' said Jake, 'but I think we can walk behind the waterfall.'

'This is totally the wrong way,' yelled Renata as Jake disappeared behind the curtain of water.

After a moment she followed him. She couldn't let him wander off alone or he'd get himself really lost.

On the other side of the waterfall, the dry stringybarks and lemon-scented gums had been replaced by towering tree ferns and huge fig trees with roots that stood up like walls.

'It doesn't make sense,' said Renata. 'There's no rainforest around here.'

'Look at this.' Jake was on his knees.

There were footprints in the muddy earth.

'Kangaroo prints,' Renata said. 'But they're huge,

way bigger than normal roo prints.' Twisted vines hung from tree branches. 'This place is creepy.' She shivered.

Jake washed his muddy hands in the creek and scooped up some water to quench his thirst. 'The water's freezing,' he said.

Renata could see his breath misting in front of him. She got out her hoodie from her backpack and put it on. 'We should go back.'

There was a drumming sound. It was getting closer. The leaves rustled. A kangaroo burst out of the trees, but not an ordinary kangaroo. It was three metres tall. With every hop it covered the length of a car. Two more giant kangaroos hopped out of the trees. Renata was so terrified she couldn't make her feet move. Jake pulled Renata behind a rock as the kangaroos moved towards the creek. One was a female. There was a leg and an ear sticking out of her pouch. The rest of the joey emerged and flopped into the mud. It was the size of a fully-grown wallaby.

'How come they're so big?' whispered Jake.

'I don't know,' Renata whispered back. 'Look at their faces.'

The kangaroos had short, blunt faces that looked

disturbingly ape-like. They bent to drink from the creek. The joey splashed at the water's edge. After every sip, the adult roos looked around and listened.

One of the vines above them started to move. Renata screamed. It wasn't a vine but a gigantic snake, black with yellow diamonds and at least six metres long. It twisted down from the tree faster than a cracking whip. It curled around the joey's legs. In seconds the joey was encircled by coils as thick as tree trunks. The adult kangaroos tried to kick the snake with their enormous feet. A forked tongue flicked out. The kangaroos crashed away into the trees. The coils around the squirming joey pulled tighter and tighter until it stopped wriggling and hung lifeless. The snake reared above its prey and opened its massive jaws. Renata couldn't take her eyes off the gruesome sight. The jaws opened wider as the giant snake swallowed the joey whole.

Renata turned and ran with Jake right behind her. They tried to retrace their steps, but even though they followed the creek, there was no sign of the waterfall.

They pushed their way through dense bush until

they came to a clearing. But they weren't alone.

A huge four-footed creature was eating leaves. It was like a wombat but the size of a cow. Renata ducked behind a tree, but the beast saw Jake. It charged at him, knocking him to the ground with its beak-like nose. It stood over Jake with one foot on his chest. Its claws cut through his windcheater. The vicious beak lowered towards Jake's face. Renata started to jump up and down, whooping and yelling. The giant wombat looked up at her, startled. So did Jake.

She waved her arms and sang the school song at the top of her voice. The wombat turned and ran.

She knelt next to Jake. 'Are you okay?'

He opened his shirt. There were deep scratches on his chest, oozing blood.

'All these animals are prehistoric,' Renata said as Jake bathed his wounds in the creek. 'It's like we've slipped back in time.'

'Are you nuts?'

'How else can you explain it?'

'We don't have to explain it,' said Jake, cupping creek water in his hands and taking another drink. 'We just have to get out of here, before we get eaten alive.'

Renata was heading back to the trees.

Jake wiped his hands on his shirt. He looked at them. There were dark hairs sprouting from the backs of his hands. He quickly stuffed them in his pockets.

The ground started to shake. A mob of giant kangaroos broke into the clearing, followed by enormous echidnas and lizard-like monsters with tusks. Renata and Jake took shelter behind a fig tree root. The animals stampeded by without even glancing at them.

'It's okay,' said Renata, trying to convince herself. 'They won't hurt us.'

'They won't,' said Jake. 'But what about that?'

A huge cat about the size of a leopard leapt out from the trees. It stopped to sniff the air.

'It can smell us,' whispered Jake.

The cat had beautiful spotted fur and large pointed ears. It also had a snarling mouth full of fangs as big as knife blades. It stalked towards them, close enough for them to smell its breath. It was bad, like rotting meat. It was making a beeline for Renata. She shrank back against a tree trunk.

Jake started rummaging in his backpack and pulled out some kebabs. 'What have you got for lunch?'

Renata looked at him as if he was going mad. Jake unzipped her pack and pulled out her lunchbox.

'Salami sandwiches. Perfect.'

Jake held out a kebab and a sandwich. 'Here, Kitty. Dinnertime.'

The cat turned its attention to Jake. He carefully moved into the clearing and put down the food. The cat padded over, sniffed it suspiciously and then started eating hungrily.

Renata was beginning to think she'd been wrong about Jake. Who would have guessed he'd turn out to be so brave?

'Let's get out of here,' Jake said.

'Has your voice broken?' Renata said as they ran away. 'It sounds really deep.'

The sound of thundering water made her find reserves of energy she didn't know she had. As they ran, Jake's shirt blew open. There were hairs growing on his chest, lots of them. He buttoned up his shirt. His stomach rumbled. The smell of the meat had made him hungry.

'We made it!' Renata shouted over the roar of the waterfall.

She felt a breath of warmer air.

'I can smell the eucalypts.'

She took a step towards the waterfall.

'Just a minute, Renata,' said a deep, growly voice behind her. 'Are you hungry?'

Renata looked at the hand that had grabbed her arm. It was covered in hair. The fingers ended in vicious claws.

'Because I am.'

Bonnikins

Sally Rippin

COME FOR a wander with me, sproggin. I have a special place to show you. It's not far, but we have to walk through the woods. Your mammy told you never to walk through the woods, did she? Well, sprog, I wouldn't worry about your mammy. She's not around now, is she? There's just me. Now, come along.

It's dark in the woods, is it deary? Well, don't you worry, your peepers will soon become accustomed. Look now, the clouds have rolled back and there shines the moon, all fullsome, upon our path. Just keep walking. It's not far now.

What's that sound, you say? Well, that be the wolves, my child. Wolves are always a-howling when the moon comes out. Don't let it fear you. Those wolves may be hungry but they're far, far away. And anyways, you be safe with me.

Keep up now, child. Don't want to be losing yerself among the leafy-tallings now, do you? The woods is no place for a child on its own. What's that? You want to go home? There now, child, that's not the voice of the sprog I know. Come along. We be nearly there. There's no going back now.

There. You see it? There. Between the leafy-tallings. Dainty innit? That be my snuggery. And a cosy one at that. But that's not what I wanted to show you. No, child, what I want you to see waits inside. Come along now, don't tarry. Ah, yes, there tis. See how the light beckons? All friendly-like? Ah, it's good to be home.

Not that I don't like yer ma and pa. No, child, it's not that. They be fine people, for sure. But I got my own sprog to care for, too. You didn't know that? Well, of course, my child. Why do you think I work so hard for yer ma and pa? You think I clean their house for fun, my sprog? No, child. I have my own sprog to feed. Yes, child.

Here we are. Come along my inchling. I hear my babe a-callin. He be hungry fer sure. Don't be fearsome, child. Why, your face be turnin' white as a bone! I thought you had more courage in you than that. What's that? You don't like that sound he's makin? He's but a babe! Sure he be noisy, but he's howlin' with hunger. You be howlin' too if you had a hunger like that.

In you go, my fingerling. Shhh! Yes, dear just like that. You don't want me to lock the door? But we must lock the door, dear. Keep the hungry beasties out. No dear, yer ma won't be calling you. She's having a nice tea now with yer pa. In a fancy dining place, innt she? She knows yer safe with me. I says to yer ma, now don't rush back, dear, yer fine sprog be safe with me! No, child, your ma and pa won't miss you for quite a bit longer.

Come along now, child. Don't pull yer hand like that. Of course it's going to hurt your wrist if you keep pulling away like that. Just be still, would you child? There's no sense in making a fuss. There! All yer kicking and screaming's upset my babe. Oh dear, child. You know it's not good to upset him. He gets awful cranky-like when he's upset. Come here, child! Don't tug. Come see my little darlin'.

Now that's not a very nice thing to say about my

baby, is it? Sure he be big, but he be no monster. He's my belov'd, aren't you, Bonnikins? Bonnikins is hungry, aren't you darling? He's just drooling because he's hungry, poor miserable thing. Look child, he's happy to see you, isn't he? There, there Bonnikins, that's better. Don't cry. Bonnikins has been waiting for his ma to come home with his dinner, hasn't he?

Mind those bones, child!

Double-you, Double-you, Double-you

Chris Miles
Illustration by Guy Holt

YOUR USERNAME and password
do not match

That's the third time
in a row.
You get your password sent to you and
check your email
Weird.
You don't remember making that
your password
You don't even know
what 'doppleganger' means.

But the new password works

Your friends are logged in
They say hi
You say hi
They ask you why you were acting so strange
today when you met them down the street
You say you didn't meet them down the street.
They want to know when they can meet those
new friends you were talking about
What new friends?
They ask you if you're really going to burn
the school down
Wh—?

There's a sound;
you've got a new message
There's no nickname or profile picture,
just seven words on your screen

'It's going to be fun
being you.'

Welcome to the home of internet

CHAT LOG IN | PEOPLE | TOPICS | GAMES | REGISTER | HELP | SEARCH

REGISTERED USER LOGIN
Please enter your password

doppleganger

Trees

George Ivanoff

JARED LOVES Karyn.

The wind howled through the trees, as Jared carved a heart around the words. The mournful sound echoed into the distance like a cry of pain. Karyn looked up into the tall branches and shivered.

Jared closed his pocket knife and tucked it back into his jeans. He sat down under the tree and patted the ground next to him.

'You shouldn't have carved that into the tree,' said Karyn, sitting down next to him.

'Why not?' asked Jared.

'It's a living thing,' she answered. 'It's not right.'

'It's a tree,' said Jared.

Karyn looked away from him and stared off into the distance.

'You know there are stories about these woods,'
she said.

'Fairy-tales!'

'Yes, some fairy-tales. But other stories too.
Mysterious disappearances. Strange happenings.
Murder!'

'I think I prefer the fairy-tales,' said Jared.

'Most of them are sad,' said Karyn.

Jared looked at her.

'You know,' she said. 'Tales of lost love and that
sort of thing... There's this story about three boys —
young men really — who fell in love with a beautiful
girl they found dancing through the woods. They were
so enamoured of her that they began to compete for
her affections. It ended in a terrible fight...'

'So?'

'Well it turns out that she was a wood nymph, and
she was trying to keep them in the enchanted forest
till sunset. At which time they were turned into trees
as punishment for bringing anger and violence into
the forest.'

'Yeah, right!'

'And that's them there,' said Karyn, pointing to the
trees ahead of them.

Jared looked up at them. They were much shorter than the other trees... in fact, they were about human size. Jared shivered. They did look kind of eerie.

Suddenly, Karyn was laughing.

'Don't worry,' she said. 'They only come to life on moonless nights.'

She laughed again.

Jared put a hand on Karyn's shoulder.

'You know,' he said. 'There's no one else around...'

He leaned in and kissed her.

As their lips met, time seemed to stand still... as if in a fairy-tale.

'Hey,' said Karyn, as she pulled back. 'It's getting dark. We'd better get back or Mum will kill me.'

'We've got plenty of time,' said Jared, reaching for her again.

But then he saw that it was indeed getting dark.

Must have lost track of time, he thought.

Karyn got to her feet and started to walk.

Jared jumped up, and immediately fell over, yelping as he felt his ankle twist. He looked down at his leg to see the end of a tree root hooked into a tear in his jeans.

'Come on,' said Karyn, playfully. 'Catch me.'

And she ran off.

'Wait!' called Jared.

But it was too late. She was gone.

Jared struggled to his feet and hobbled after her. The woods seemed denser than before, the branches more difficult to get through. He stumbled, a thorny branch tearing another hole in his jeans and scratching his leg. Jared tried to increase his pace, ignoring the pain in his ankle, but the trees and bushes seemed to be closing in on him.

He began to panic, thrashing his arms around and trying to run. But he kept tripping over tree roots and hitting into branches. It was as if the roots were coming up out of the ground, deliberately trying to trip him. It was as if the branches were trying to grab him. And it was now so dark, he could barely see where he was going.

Suddenly Jared yelped as something caught his arm and held it firm. A branch? A hand? He tried to struggle but it only gripped more fiercely. Twigs and branches seemed to be all around him... clawing at him... grabbing him... holding him down.

He twisted his arm around and reached into his pocket for the knife, intending to slash his way free...

but it wasn't there. Had it slipped from his pocket? Then suddenly, there it was in front of him... caught in a branch... held tight in its twiggy grasp. A strong gust of wind made the branch sway, thrusting the knife towards him.

As Karyn ran out onto the path, she heard the eerie howl of the wind echoing through the trees... like a scream of pain.

'Jared!' she called.

No answer.

She looked around nervously, wondering if she should go back to look for him, or just wait. Then she heard frantic footfalls and ragged sobbing. Seconds later, Jared stumbled out from bushes clutching his bleeding arm. He collapsed onto the ground in front of her, shaking and panting, a mad fear in his eyes.

'Your arm,' cried Karyn. 'What happened to your arm?'

She knelt down beside him, and pulled away his hand.

Carved into the flesh of his shoulder was a large bloody heart.

And within it were the words Jared loves Karyn.

The Dreams of Aunty Morbid

James Moloney

MY FATHER left when I was young
leaving me with just my Mum.
She loves me dearly, that I know
but still it came as quite a blow
when she announced her crafty plan
to find herself another man.
'I need some time without you, dear.'
About the rest she wasn't clear.

When Mother told me of her scheme,
to tell the truth, I wasn't keen
to spend the summer on my own.
'But Mother, I'll be so alone!'
I told her as she packed my bag.
'So many weeks will drag and drag.'

She shook her head and smoothed my hair
and promised as she drove me there,
'You will have a lovely time,
living with this aunt of mine.'

But from the start I wasn't sure
when Old Aunt Morbid shut the door
and led me to my room up high.
(The staircase seemed to reach the sky.)
My window overlooked a wood
and sparsely-peopled neighbourhood.
At dinner Morbid said but little
except that I should eat my vittles
'Then to bed so you can sleep,'
she said, 'and so there's not a peep
from you while in your playful dreams
I have a story book that seems
to help my guests enjoy their slumber,
lie back now and pick a number.'
A story couldn't do me harm.
'Seven is my lucky charm,'
I told her, feeling somnolent.
She smiled and whispered, 'Excellent.'

With just a candle by the bed,
old Aunt Morbid sat and read
of demons, ghouls and apparitions
and cloak-clad Counts with poor dentition
who rode the clouds in dark of night
in search of tender throats to bite.
And let me straight away admit
that I was terrified by it.
'Please stop,' I begged of Old Aunt Morbid.
But nothing that I said or did
could stay her 'til she reached the last
and oh! By then the die was cast.

Rising to her feet again,
she stepped towards the window pane
and with the pages open still
she placed the book upon the sill.
'Time to dream,' was all she'd say
and so Aunt Morbid slipped away
leaving me in darkest gloom
watched through glass by ghostly moon.
No sooner did I close my eyes
than started up the deathly cries
of wolves on distant hills a-howl

and thirsty creatures on the prowl.
I dared not move, my throat was dust
but take a look I knew I must
at spectres dangling from the roof
and dripping blood from every tooth.
And though the window stayed shut tight
those phantoms breached my room all right
to hover grisly, grim and dead
a single foot above my bed.

'Wake up, I moaned, it's just a dream'
but all that night their silent scream
kept me from a moment's rest
until the dawn's pale light caressed
the window of my blighted room
to chase away these beasts of doom
The ghouls' attack at last was thwarted.
I stumbled from my room exhausted
and all that Aunty Mo would say
was, 'Hello, dear, enjoy your day.'

Every night when I retreated
to my room the fiends repeated
gruesome tricks and deeds that taunted

'til my mind grew weak and haunted.
Muscles ached, my eyes were red,
another week and I'd be dead.
I had to stop those wretched knaves
or see my corpse among the graves.
Then, huddled tight to contemplate
my dwindling life and wretched fate
my eye alighted on that book.
It seemed to me that every spook
was conjured from its wicked pages
to set about its nightly rages.
I saw at once it was the key,
the only way to rescue me.
I grabbed it from the window ledge
and made myself a little pledge.
If I survive this nightly horror
Morbid's going to pay, begorra!

When ghostly spectres filled the air
they found me calmly lying there.
They floated near with face contorted
unaware they'd soon be thwarted.
The book lay open on my lap
I jerked it closed with upward snap

James Moloney

'I've got you all, you fiendish hounds,'
and from the book most fearful sounds
erupted loud and furious
as creatures cruel and spurious
did their best to wriggle free
but I had plans for these banshee.

I crept towards Old Morbid's door
until I heard her sniff and snore.
She's fast asleep, that's good for me.
I slipped inside possessed by glee.
'You'd love a story Aunty Mo
I'm sure you would, let's have a go.'
The book, by now, had ceased to shake
and swiftly, so she wouldn't wake,
I turned the pages 'til I spied
a tale that left me satisfied
of ghastly trolls and vampire's teeth
and poltergeists upon the heath.
The words were grisly. 'Oh what fun,'
I whispered on 'til it was done.
The book I left beside her bed
pages open, then I fled.

Much later as I settled in,
there came a loud and mighty din.
Along the hall from Morbid's room
shouts of fear and deepest doom
rose up the stairwells high and steep
and to that sound, I fell asleep.

Mr Magnifico's Amazing Moving Photos

Amy Hawley

'**THIS PLACE** really needs to get some new rides or something,' Eric complained. He tipped a handful of Smarties into his mouth and screwed up his nose. 'These taste ancient.'

'And yet you're still eating them,' Sophie said, slanting an eyebrow.

Eric shrugged. 'Who turns down candy?'

They walked through the modest crowd of fair goers. The neighbourhood carnival was the same jumping castle, merry-go-round and haunted train ride it was every year and there were only so many times you could shove ping-pong balls into the mouths of plastic clown heads before the water pistol prize just wasn't as rewarding as it used to be.

'Wait. What's that thing?' Sophie said, looking

at something ahead. Eric looked up from his candy showbag.

They came to a windowless booth they'd never seen before.

'Mr Magnifico's Amazing Moving Photos,' Sophie read from the painted sign outside. 'Yeah, right. Wanna check it out?'

'Whatever,' Eric said, crunching down on some more Smarties.

They pulled aside the curtain and walked inside.

'Whoa,' Sophie breathed, heading towards a wall of framed photos. 'They are moving.'

Eric looked up at the photos. In each one was a boy or girl looking around or pacing back and forth in front of a shadowy blue backdrop.

Sophie was gazing up with gaping mouth. 'It's like something out of Harry Potter.'

'They're probably just like those digital photo frames you can get,' Eric said sceptically. He looked around the inside of the stall. Each wall was covered with a black curtain. There was nothing else in the room but Sophie, the wall of photos and himself.

'I dunno. If they are just digital recordings there's no way you could get me to look as scared as that.'

Sophie was peering at a photo of a boy who seemed to be banging on the front of the photo, shouting desperately at the top of his lungs.

Suddenly one of the curtains was pulled aside and a man stepped through wearing a long black coat.

'I thought I heard customers,' said Mr Magnifico. 'Come to have your photo taken?'

'I guess,' said Sophie. 'How much is it?'

'Five dollars,' said the man, clapping his hands eagerly.

Sophie turned to Eric. 'What d'ya reckon?'

'Hey, do what you like. It's your money,' said Eric.

'Okay,' said Sophie. She handed Mr Magnifico some money.

The man pocketed the coins and his eyes glinted with anticipation. 'Right this way.' He pulled back the curtain for Sophie to go through. Eric went to follow but Mr Magnifico held out a hand. 'One at a time, please.'

'Fine. I'll wait out here,' Eric shrugged.

Sophie was only gone for a minute when she walked back through the curtain.

'So what happened? Did you have to act like a moron?' Eric asked.

Sophie shook her head and pouted casually. 'Nope. Just had to stand there while he took my photo.'

The curtain was pulled aside again and out came Mr Magnifico holding a photo frame. He presented it to Sophie. 'Here you are. Came out rather well.'

Sophie and Eric peered over the photo and Eric had to duck away because Sophie jumped in alarm. There she was in the photo, eyes wide, features twisted in horror and her hands planted right up against the picture. It looked like she was shouting something.

'Yikes,' Sophie muttered after a while. 'You gonna get one?'

She was looking at Eric with a grin. Her shock seemed to have worn off quickly. Eric suspected she had put on a show for the camera just to freak him out.

'Pfft. I guess.' Eric gave Mr Magnifico some money and then followed him through the curtain.

'Just stand in front of the screen there. That's it.' Mr Magnifico ducked behind an old-looking camera on a tripod. He pulled a black sheet over himself. 'Smile.'

Eric didn't bother smiling. He was just going to look bored in his photo. He certainly wasn't going to put on a show like Sophie had.

There was a click and a blinding flash. Eric blinked repeatedly, bubbles of light blooming and popping in front of his eyes. When the light finally melted away he looked around. His heart leapt in his chest. His breath caught in his throat. His skin went ice cold.

In front of him was a large screen. He could see Mr Magnifico and his camera. But he could also see himself. Mr Magnifico was ushering him back out through the curtain.

'Hey!' Eric ran to the screen but he thumped against it. A bite of panic snapped around the back of his neck. He pushed against the screen but it was solid as rock. 'Hey! Wait!'

Eric looked around frantically and gasped when he saw the vast darkness all around him. He spun around and saw that the shadow blue backdrop was still there behind him. Everywhere else was pitch black. He turned back to the screen through which he could see Mr Magnifico, who suddenly looked very large and had his arms stretched past the edge of the screen.

Eric watched it like a movie. For a moment it looked like an arm was covering the whole screen.

Then he was looking up at himself and Sophie. Their enormous heads were looking down at him.

And Eric could only stare back.

The Lane

Stephen Whiteside

THE LANE is dark and narrow.
A dim lamp lights the scene.
I see the doorway where my parents
Recently have been.

The night air suddenly seems chill;
A creeping sense of dread.
I hear an owl hoot softly.
A bat flies overhead.

The lane seems somehow strangely changed,
And yet not changed at all.
Where now are all the people,
And that busy road-side stall?

I walk towards the doorway.
I'll surely find them soon.
A single star shines faint beside
A narrow rim of moon.

I open wide the heavy door
I'm dizzy, feeling sick.
For where once led a passage
Stands a wall of solid brick!

Lunar Rose

Susanne Gervay

Illustration by Tegan Bell

I DON'T want a birthday party this year except my
'best' friend Carla harasses me.

'You have to. Thirteen is the big one.'

I give in, as always.

Carla is fourteen already. She used to be skinny
with a cute smile. Now she's stunning with deep
green eyes and long blonde hair that swings as she
sways her hips. My hair is still short wavy brown
and my eyes are shadowy. Everyone's changed since
they've turned thirteen. I don't want to change.
Thirteen is an unlucky number.

The party.

Carla and I spend all day getting the garden cabin
ready with balloons, streamers, glow-in-the-dark

moons and stars. Carla's funny as she dances around on tip-toes pretending to be a movie star. We laugh and the knot in my stomach softens.

'The party'll be fun,' Carla promises. 'You're thirteen today.'

I was born one minute before midnight.

'A miracle baby,' Mum says.

My parents weren't supposed to have babies. On the day I was due, my mother was crying. I was coming too quickly, too soon. My father drove wildly to the hospital, but he didn't make it. He stopped the car to help my mum and a rose garden just seemed to appear. I was born under the moon. It was a difficult birth, but the moon let me go. Mum thanks the moon ever since. She named me Lunar Rose.

Carla and I are getting ready together which means Carla spending three hours putting make up on, throwing dresses and tops onto the floor. She's checking out the thirteenth pair of earrings. I bury myself in my quilt, listening to Carla ranting about the boys she hates, the boys she loves, hates, loves, hates, loves. My head's a mess. I don't want to be thirteen. I slip into my gossamer skirt and petal blouse.

Mum and Dad are sitting on wooden chairs outside the house. They're the security — the bodyguards, bouncers and heavy-duty team. Mum's wearing her fluffy caramel tracksuit and looks like an exploding sausage. Dad thinks he's tough wearing his desperate woolly grey sleeveless jacket. He feels his woolly jacket.

'Cool,' he winks.

Sure, if he was a sheep.

Mum giggles because she really believes he looks cool.

I love my parents but I sometimes wonder if we're born on the same planet. They're so different to me. I couldn't stop laughing when Mum told me about her teenage birthday parties where they played charades, the limbo and danced to the Village People's YMCA.

Mum and Dad are determined that there'll be no gate crashers at my party. Cars slow down when they hear the music and see balloons. Then they spot the woolly jacket security team and zoom off beeping or laughing, although I thought a figure in black jeans slipped in.

Or maybe it was trees in the flickering moonlight.

Carla waits for the right moment then flounces

into the garden cabin with me tagging behind her.
The music's blaring but no one is dancing. Boys are
stuck like mud in one corner and the girls in another.
Carla spots a cute guy, then disappears outside. A few
guys and girls connect up. The music is loud.

It's hot inside so I wander into the garden. The
moon is golden yellow. The roses smell like honey
and I move towards them. I see Dad carrying the
blazing birthday cake decorated with moons and
roses. Mum's trailing behind him. Carla dances back
into the cabin with the cute guy.

'Lunar Rose, Lunar Rose' floats across the
flowerbeds.

I want to go back into the cabin, but suddenly the
moonlight catches me. The honey scent is trickling
into my throat and I can't speak. My friends are
calling me and I want to go inside, but I can't.

My heart is thudding. Thorns are scraping my skin.
I struggle to get up, but the moonbeams stun me. I
want my father's woolly arms to hold me and my
mother to stroke my cheek. Carla's voice pierces my
ears. 'Lunar Rose.' I'm trying to get to her. I want to
hear her gossip about boys and how she loves and

hates them. But there's only the moon, hands, black jeans, another planet and shadows grasping. My eyes close.

One minute to midnight. The music stops. The candles burn out. Carla's screams pierce the dark. Dad wildly searches for me. Mum is crying.

Midnight.

Thirteen.

Gone.

Don't Jump

Robyne Young

DON'T JUMP! yells Greg
Echoes the signs we all ignore;
Put up by the old farts who run the town.

What a girl! We yell back at him
Lifting our bodies from the bridge
And into air, pulling our knees and heads
Into our chests and
For a moment freeze...
Eyes closed.
Waiting.

Drop down.
Still curled, hit the water.
Stings like hell then sink in black and cold.

Stretch out. Reach up.
And up.....And up........
Break through the water, breathe.
But something has my legs.
Arms reach for sun.
Fingers barely pierce the surface.

Pulled down. Can't see. Too dark.
Tired from kicking this thing
That's tackling harder than a player
    in a rugby game.
Sight clears. Eyes focus.
Greg? Greg?

Too strong. Give in.
Two words echo.
Don't jump.

All U Can Eat

Ananda Braxton-Smith

KITCHENER STUFFIT was the fattest kid in school. And he wasn't fat because of glands, either; he was fat because he never knowingly ate anything but fat.

'Fat is good,' he would say with a smile. 'It's what carries the flavour.'

His favourite flavours for the fat were salt, or sugar.

Kitchener liked to start his day with two breakfasts, like a hobbit. Lunch was a two-foot bread stick crammed with three types of meat. He loved combining meats. Snacks — such as wedges-with-grated-cheese-and-a-dipping-sauce, or hash-browns-between-two-curry-pies — kept him going until dinnertime.

In a playground milling with shop-bought, off-the-rack, regular clothing Kitchener Stuffit alone was dressed in tailor-mades from Teen Titan or Prince of the Realm. His shirts flapped like sails in any small breeze, around pants the shape of hot-air balloons, above sneakers resembling canoes.

Every recess, Kitchener would sail into the playground, clothing billowing around him like a galleon in a grey sea, and devour his three-meat bread stick. Tiny Year 7s hid behind the wheelie bins, and watched as he chug-a-lugged two litres of choc milk showing every sign of pleasure, and not one sign of shame.

Gangs of skinny, rat-like guys threw pebbles at his stomach to see if he could feel it. They snuck bras into his sports bag. They called him names like Meatbag, Girlyman and Chunk. Among these many part-time tormentors, there were three regulars for whom Kitchener was a hobby. The three boys, Jonno, Nicko and Tran, came to feed at his self-esteem every chance they had. They gorged on Kitchener's heart. They feasted on his embarrassment. Or rather, they would have if Kitchener Stuffit had had the decency to be embarrassed. But he wasn't.

When Jonno, Nicko and Tran insulted him, he just smiled in his distracted way. When he found a bra in his bag, he laughed. When they threw pebbles at him, he actually stuck out his belly and batted them away. Not only was he not embarrassed, Kitchener seemed happy.

Year 9 was Kitchener's biggest year. From a mere habitat he grew into a planet, complete with three mean-as-a-cut-snake tormentor moons, and rings of tiny Year 7 space-dust. On Little Buddy Day he provided shade for at least five or six little buddies. The science teacher, Mr Sudden, said Kitchener should always go in the pool first, so that he didn't keep 'displacing' the juniors.

Even Music-Theatre-Guy didn't attract the same amount of attitude.

Then the school held a Champion Chef competition. The judges were two TV cooks and an ex-minister of agriculture. Mrs Fledge and the cooking classes hunkered down, and the smells drifting around the school made people stop in the playground and look up, hopefully, at the steamy Food & Nutrition windows. Kitchener spent all his

time staring into space and muttering to himself.
'Apple-soaked pork,' he'd whisper. 'Cheddar-lined-crackling', or, following a long shuddering breath,
'Bacon-wrapped sugar-ribs'. He scribbled a lot of notes
in a gravy-stained notebook.

The championship arrived and Kitchener won the
Savoury award. The judges were quietly impressed
by his size, and were charmed by his escort of tiny
Year 7s. They were unable to resist his Three-Meat
Wrap w/Cheese-of-Your-Choice (a masterstroke, said
the minister) and his own Home-Made Extra-Creamy
Mayonnaise.

He would have won the Sweet trophy too. His
entry was waiting, pastry puffed and layered, triple
cream whipped and nebulous, dark and white
chocolate surprises nestled inside their marshmallow
pillows. Only the Tim-Tams needed adding. But
Jonno, Nicko and Tran had had enough of Kitchener's
success.

When Kitchener went to add the final touches to
Mount Pudding he found it defaced by three poops,
three human poops, forming a K at the peak where
the Tim-Tams were to have gone. Tiny Year 7s reeled
back. His mother gagged. The judges commiserated.

It was 'sheer vandalism', they said, and not only 'uncalled for', but 'entirely inappropriate'.

More importantly, though, it was the first time Kitchener didn't smile. Finally, he got it. Jonno, Nicko and Tran were content.

It was a new Kitchener who returned to school on Monday. He took on running the All U Can Eat stall at the annual fundraising fete but this time there were no smiles, no dreaming or planning; there was only this serious, determined big guy. The tiny Year 7s vanished from his orbit. Concerned teachers became less concerned.

'Good.' They nodded knowingly at each other. 'All that happiness was just a front. Now he'll get realistic about himself.'

The whole school community turned out for the fete. Kitchener's All U Can Eat was the star stall. Parents, teachers, students and welcome guests clustered in sighing groups to feast. There were only three absences. Jonno, Nicko and Tran didn't turn up. Nobody much missed them.

By early afternoon Kitchener had run out of his signature dish with all the delicious trimmings, known from now on as Stuffit's Three-Meat Wrap.

Regret

A. Seib

'I'VE BEEN thinking a lot lately, about things I've said or done that might have hurt you.' Amanda brushes at her pale cheeks, tears glistening in the sunlight that streams into my bedroom window. 'You would think that after all these years I'd know what they were,' she continues. 'I've never been too sure, but I think I've figured some out.'

I follow her gaze as she stares through my window. Her eyes are fixed on the tyre that swings from our Jacaranda. I drift to the opposite side of the room and slouch on the floor. There's no room on my bed since she dumped all her clothes on it.

'Remember the times I barged ahead of you and hopped onto that tyre-swing?' Amanda asks. 'Just because I was faster and I knew you'd give up and I'd have it all to myself.' She blows her nose into a handful of pink tissues.

When she speaks again, her head is down and her voice is soft. 'That was selfish and I'm sorry. I never meant to hurt you.'

I roll my eyes and wonder how long this will last. She slides onto the stool in front of the mirror and fingers everything on my dresser — photos, trophies, jewellery. I watch her pluck up a brush — my brush. She pulls it through her long, dark hair. Then she pauses, stroking her fingers down the brush bristles.

'I should never have laughed at your singing either.' She sniffs. 'The concert… when you forgot the words to that song. I should've supported you, not laughed.' She shivers, rubbing her arms. 'I said you'd never be a singer.' Amanda's face tightens, then she whispers, 'That was horrid. I'm so, so, sorry.'

I remember that night and wish she hadn't brought it up.

Amanda sighs and stands, folds her arms and peers at her feet. She's a statue for a full minute, just staring down. I can't ever remember her saying this many words to me in a whole week, let alone one day.

Finally, she shuffles across the room, opens the wardrobe and pulls some jeans from a hanger. My wardrobe. My best jeans.

I used to offer her my things all the time and she never once wanted them. Now she takes them every day. That's my second favourite shirt she's squishing into. The one I bought at Skylarks with my birthday money.

'I wish I didn't have to do this without you,' Amanda says. 'I never realised how much it meant to have you there until I thought about standing on stage alone.'

We worked on a fundraising project together and won the Principal's community award that's presented at the end of year school assembly. Amanda's going without me. Those are my earrings she's wearing, and my shoes she's jamming onto her feet, even though they give her blisters.

Amanda glances in the mirror again and clears her throat. 'I'm sorry about the time I spilt cocoa on your watercolour and told you it was a stupid painting and to stop crying like a baby.'

I stand as she turns to pick up my backpack. I follow her from the room, sticking close to her heels the whole way down the stairs, through the front door and along our path.

She drags my bike from the garage. From behind our front gate I watch her peddle away — a clone of me. I can't help wonder why it still bugs me that she's using all my things.

It's not like I can, now that I'm dead.

Behind Our Backs

Sally Odgers

Since time began the Shivers, lurking,
Hide behind the human back
In and out their fingers working
Venturesomely to attack.
Evil? Hardly! Simply spooky
Rippled chills upon the spine
Slipping, stretching, somewhat kooky
Reaching for your neck – or mine.
Even now I feel a shudder
Vibrating from heel to head
Inside out I hear it judder
Hush! Don't look! Don't look! I
Said.

Ghostwriter

Stephanie Campisi

NIGHT AT the farmhouse is the colour of spilt ink. It drapes around you like black velvet, and when you wave your hands in front of your face you see nothing unless there's a full moon whitewashing the world and drawing long, withered shadows in its wake.

Tonight there is a moon, but the sky is thick with lurking clouds that catch at it, blotting its round face from view before releasing it.

It is dark.

And when it is dark you hear things.

Wedged beneath the blankets, where your grandmother has tucked you with kindly intent, your only useful sense is your hearing. You hear the hum of a mosquito, like a high-pitched kazoo, and the hot water service that belches water along the pipes with a pained gasp.

And you hear the thoughtful clatter of typewriter keys, heavy and slow.

It sounds like the cracking of knuckles.

The noise trickles down in sentence-length bursts from the attic, which is full of dusty sheets cloaking rotten furniture and racks of faded clothes. It is impossible that anyone can be up there, because you can hear the faint rumble of the television, which means that your mother and grandmother are still awake, sipping at their wine and rubbing the belly of the cat with their slippered feet.

Or at least, it should be impossible.

You know that your grandfather had been a writer. But your last memory of him involves your whole family wearing clothes the colour of a moonless night.

Your grandmother still has the faded newspapers and the bent magazines in which his stories appeared. There are a few books, too, very thin and pale and wedged between the set of encyclopaedias. Their edges are warped and curling from where you once knocked over a glass of water. They dried, but strangely, like a broken bone that is never quite the same again. But before his death he had not written a word for years. Or rather, things had been written, but he claimed he had not been the one writing them.

His last stories had all been horror. This is why the typewriter is in the attic.

The clacking sound is like a dripping tap. It is impossible to ignore, and the more you try, the more it needles into your brain until it is all you can think of. You count the clacks like they are Morse code.

The moon escapes the cotton-wool clutches of a cloud, and scuds across the sky, its glowing skin casting a sheen that illuminates the garden and trickles through your window. You listen intently. The typing is quieter, more subdued, but it still sounds like the cracking of marbles.

You feel bolder now that you can see, and you can still hear the fake laughter from the television and the clinking of a wine glass against your grandmother's heavy jewellery. They reassure you, these everyday things.

You slide out of bed, your bare feet curling against the frigid lino, and pad towards the attic. Your feet are clammy, and they leave damp marks against the patterned floor.

Now you are beneath the attic, and hear not only the chattering of the typewriter keys, but the cheerful ping every now and then that means the end of a line of type has been reached. From the attic trapdoor swings a thin cord, like a hair from a cobweb.

Your heart keeps time with the clacks. Or perhaps it is the other way around.

You jump to catch the cord, then draw down the trapdoor. The folded ladder swings down, shivering nervously by your feet. Its rungs are like tree bark against your hands, but you barely worry about splinters.

You climb, your hands and feet moving to the rhythm of the typing.

The attic is carpeted with dust and dressed with mildewed tarp. Except for the typewriter, which sits stately and glossy on a rickety table. Its body is black and gleaming like a beetle, and the golden tendons that fill its front like teeth bob up and down as its keys depress, one by one.

'Hello?' It's barely a whisper, and the faint sound curls around you like a cat. You take a step forward, peering at the moon-shadowed sheet of paper that lolls forward under its own weight.

Hello.

The typewriter pings, and shifts down a line.

'Grandad?'

No.

The typewriter pings.

You take a step back, but your eyes, wide and staring, can still see the next line of text, clear and bold, just before the moon vanishes again —

The Strange Bird

Gabrielle Wang

ON A DAY of wild storm, a strange bird
   blew into my garden,
eyes like emeralds, feathers as golden
   as Pharaoh's throne.
Vermilion and ochre and all the colours of life
   played in its plumage.
Its eyes caught mine, looked deep into my soul.
I could not turn away.
Lifting its head against the rain, the bird called a
   call that filled me with longing.
Suddenly, a harsh wail pierced the rain.
We turned.
At the top of an old pine at the end of the garden,
   perched on a naked branch, there lurked a
   looming shadow.

Its dark wings were like two empty coffins.
Who had it come for?
The strange golden bird looked at me.
The dark shadow leered and stretched greedily
    in my direction.
Terror gripped my body and I began to tremble.
My limbs felt cold and rigid.
Then in a flash, off into the rain-soaked sky
    the strange bird flew, its call beckoning
    the dark shadow to follow.
As the grey sky swallowed them up, fear passed
    and left me, alone;
    the rain salty on my face.

Gone Fishing

Rebecca Hayman

WAVES LAP against the old jetty. Dad lowers himself into the canoe after me and we push off. After twenty minutes paddling, Dad stops.

'This'll do us, I reckon. We don't want to go too far out in case the wind gets up.' He baits my line and hands it to me.

Dad has never taken me out on the lake before. He always said it was too dangerous.

'Never know when the wind'll get up,' he says.

Suddenly there's a tug at my line.

'I've got one,' I say.

Dad leans forward to help. 'Nice and easy.'

Bit by bit, I wind in the line until the fish surfaces. Dad is quick with the net and scoops it into the canoe.

'Wow, she's a beauty!'

'She's a whopper. You did good to reel her in.'

At that moment the sun dips below the horizon. I look up.

'Dad?' I say. I can hardly see the jetty, it's so far away. 'We'd better get back.'

We pack away the lines and turn the canoe for home. I dip my paddle in the water and pull in time with Dad. But nothing happens. Or worse than nothing. We keep drifting in the other direction.

'Must be the wind,' Dad says and pulls harder.

For five minutes we paddle furiously but it's no use. We're still drifting the other way.

'I can't do it, Dad.'

'We'll have to head straight to shore and then hug the coast. Bit further. But not to worry.' We turn for the shore, but now we are just drifting sideways.

'Paddle harder,' Dad yells.

But I'm paddling as hard as I can, my arms and shoulders are burning. I stop. Dad stops too, and the canoe swivels to face the way it is drifting, right towards a stretch of land jutting out into the lake. I can see the tea-tree and the pink of pigface flowers. Reeds grow at the water's edge.

The canoe drifts ever closer and then noses in and nudges the shore.

'Might as well stretch our legs,' Dad says.

I clamber over the front and hold the canoe for Dad. He looks around and rubs his hands together. 'Good thing you caught that fish. We'll cook it up and head back when the wind drops.'

I nod. There is no wind.

I push in among the tea-tree, looking for wood for the fire. There's a crack. It sounds like a gunshot.

'Dad!' I run back out. 'What was that?'

He laughs. 'Bet you stood on a stick.'

The fish cooks quickly on the coals and we pick over it with our fingers. Dad throws the carcass in the fire and then adds some more branches. The flames rise, crackle, hiss and die down. It's then I realise Dad's gone.

'Dad?' I struggle to my feet. 'Dad!'

'What?' He pushes back through the undergrowth. 'I was just washing my hands in the lake. You should wash up too.'

I shake my head. I'm not going anywhere. A cry rises from the bush.

'What's that?'

'Just a curlew, you know, a type of water bird.' He pats the ground next to him and I shuffle over. Behind me there's a moan. I twist my head but see only darkness.

'Just the tea-trees rubbing against each other,' Dad says.

There's another crack and then the sound of running. It's like I can feel it in the earth. A trembling. I jump to my feet.

'Wallabies,' Dad says.

I feel silly and sit apart from him. I'll show him I'm not afraid. Then a great crying starts up, far away and then closer and then all around. I press against Dad's body.

'Black cockatoos,' he's saying as the crying fades.

Then there is a sound like a man sobbing.

'Lyrebird,' Dad says and I know for sure he's lying. 'They imitate sounds,' he says.

Sure. But they live in the mountains. Not here. Finally the sobbing fades and there is silence.

'I think the wind has dropped,' Dad says.

What wind? I follow him back to the canoe and we push off from the shore.

We can see a light and we head towards it, our

progress effortless, and within half an hour we're at the jetty. The light is the lantern of an old fisherman.

'Out late,' he says.

'Head wind,' Dad grunts.

The old man nods. 'Got taken to the point, hey?' He juts his chin out into the darkness. 'Dead Man's Finger.'

'Is that what it's called?' I whisper.

The fisherman smiles. 'Get a fright did you, son? Crazy old black fella lived out there. Used to say his people were murdered. Used to cry like a baby. Silly old coot.' The fisherman sniffs. 'He died years ago. There's nothing living out there now.'

'Except a lot of birds,' I say.

The Dream

Angela Vernon

LIGHTS OUT. Darkness descends.
Bury your head beneath the sheet.
Though you try, you cannot stop it —
reluctantly you fall asleep.

And there it is — the dream.
Slipping and slithering it comes.
Through the damp and the dark it takes you —
there is nowhere for you to run.

And so you find yourself
in a place of shadows and gloom,
with the smell of death and decay
and the taste of fear and doom.

Moonlight shifts and flickers
making shadows, deception and lies.
You know this place; you've been here before
it's where the dead things rise.

Tombstones lying side by side,
between the rows you tread.
As the ground begins to tremble
your heart is filled with dread.

The ground heaves and tears
wailing and moaning, the silence shatters.
And then come the dead things
all dust and rags and tatters.

Bones rattling they rise
from each and every grave.
Cold hands reaching for you –
it's your breath, your life they crave.

Closer and closer they stagger,
staring with empty eyes.
Hungry mouths a-gaping,
breathing with tortured sighs.

The dead ones surround you,
things of hunger and of greed.
Clutching, suffocating you –
it's your trembling soul they need.

You try to run but cannot,
your feet are rooted to the ground.
You open your mouth to scream,
but cannot make a sound.

But in your head there's a whisper
'Good night, sleep well Little One'
drawing you back from the darkness.
you find the strength to run.

Icy fingers claw your back,
angry wails fill the stagnant air.
Never, ever should you look back –
keep going, you're almost there.

You wake, your heart is pounding,
still breathing, but only just.
In your nostrils the smell of decay,
in your mouth the taste of dust.

Corn Dolly Dead

Sheryl Gwyther

THERE WERE hundreds laid out in neat, golden rows in the display cabinets, hanging by their necks in the shop window, twirling in the air conditioner's draft.

'What are they?' I pointed through the glass.

'They're corn dollies,' Joan Pringle said. 'We plait the last wheat sheaves of the season — sometimes in that human shape, but sometimes in circles and spirals — and sometimes we bury them in the ground to honour the Corn Goddess.'

We continued along Solstice's main street. I didn't comment on the fact the town was surrounded by wheat fields, not corn.

Something niggled in my mind about that Corn

Dolly shop. It wasn't the only strange thing I'd come across since arriving on the bus a week ago.

'Why so many corn dollies, Joan?'

The woman smiled. 'They're popular with tourists.'

I looked around. 'I don't see any tourists.'

There wasn't even a motel in town.

'We don't encourage them to stay. They buy their corn dollies and move on to other places. That's the way we like it here in Solstice. The ceremonial burning of the Corn Dolly is of no interest to outsiders.'

It was hard to miss the giant corn dolly. It stood in the field near the Pringle's home, a human form as tall as a house, made from woven wicker.

Joan ploughed along the street and I rushed to catch up.

'One more stop,' she said.

At Tom's Hardware the owner greeted Joan and nodded at me. 'Welcome to Solstice, Leah.'

'You know my name?'

'Everyone knows who you are.' He handed me a chocolate bar from the drink fridge. 'We're so excited about Joan and Matthew fostering a city girl.'

I smiled.

Maybe living in the country wouldn't be so bad.

'What's your height, dearie?' Tom said.

I shrugged.

He pulled out a tape measure. 'May I?'

I let him.

'One fifty centimetres. Perfect,' he said. The tape flicked back into its case.

Since arriving in Solstice the adults I'd met had talked in riddles — usually over my head like I was a child.

'Come, Leah.' Joan hustled me from the shop. 'It's time to wash your hair and prepare for the banquet tonight.'

'What banquet?'

'To celebrate the harvest,' she said. Her eyes gleamed. 'You'll see when the time comes. Now you must rest.'

With nothing else to do I lay on my bed, listening to the buzz of cicadas.

I woke before sunset. In the field near the house, the shadow of the huge corn dolly rippled across the furrows. Someone had piled dead branches around its legs.

I put on my new dress. Its golden silkiness shimmered in the light as I slipped it over my head.

Joan had insisted I unbraid and brush out my hair, so to please her, I did. It rippled across my shoulders, like the wheat fields they all seemed to love.

Before we left, she gave me a glass of sweet ginger beer, made from her own recipe, she said.

'Come, child,' Matthew beckoned me through the front door. 'It's time.'

We walked through the gate to the field.

In the torchlight I sensed the presence of others. We neared the wicker corn dolly and several bonfires were lit. Then I saw them — the men, women and children of Solstice. They stared at me, their eyes glittering in the fire light.

As Matthew led me into the circle they began to chant. *Accept our sacrifice. Bless our harvest, Corn Goddess. Accept our sacrifice.*

The sacrifice to the Corn Goddess, their giant, wicker corn dolly, was it to be me?

I struggled, but Matthew gripped my wrist. A man moved forward with a burning stick and touched the base of the corn dolly. The flames flickered, then spread through the dry timber.

Relief swept through me and I sank to my knees.

I was not their sacrifice.

'Dance with us, Leah. Rejoice, for you will be reborn!'

So I danced — a crazy, abandoned, wild dance. The townfolk circled the flames of their wicker Corn Goddess, clapping and chanting.

Then my legs grew heavy. I stumbled, but before I fell, the Pringles were there; their arms strong and supporting. Heat spread through my veins.

I gasped. The ginger beer's sweetness had disguised something else.

In the flicker of firelight they carried me across the field. The crowd parted and I saw in the ground a freshly dug hole; beside it lay a woven wicker case.

Joan nodded. 'See, my dear, it's a perfect fit for you.'

The chanting swelled again as they sang to the Corn Goddess, begging her to accept their corn dolly sacrifice for the promise of more bountiful harvests.

Suddenly, they stopped and turned to me.

Silence.

Except for my thumping heart...

One Dark and Stormy Night, at a Boarding School Near You...

Meredith Costain

Illustration by Marc McBride

YOU'D BETTER take a look
'Cos you don't know who they took
When they came for their midnight feast.

A scrabbling of claws –
A slathering of jaws –
A whiff of breath that reeked of beast.

They went round all the beds
Inspecting toes and heads
Searching for a tasty treat.

Meredith Costain

Then pounced upon their prey
And carried him away
Back to their lair to eat.

The Gift

Barry Jonsberg

'I CAN'T believe you'd do this!'

He stood at the kitchen sink, head bowed, luggage scattered over the floor. Why did it always have to be this way, every time he returned from a business trip? He'd been home two minutes and she wanted to argue. Well, he was jet-lagged and the deal had fallen through. If it was an argument she wanted…

'It's Briony's fifth birthday. I got her a present. What's the big deal?'

'You really don't know, do you?' Her arms were crossed, her face set. 'A doll, Alan? ' She shook her head. 'Unbelievable.'

'She's five. What did you expect me to buy? A power saw?'

Their voices were rising, word by word. The air sparked with resentment.

'You would've bought her a power saw if she'd been a boy. So sexist! Hey, it's the twenty-first century, in case you hadn't noticed. How about joining it?'

Alan felt his jaw setting. A pulse beat above his right eye.

'Well, Briony loves it. You saw her reaction. Maybe you should forget your feminist gibberish for one moment and just be happy for her.'

It had cost enough. The latest advance in interactive toys. Incredibly life-like, with an in-built microprocessor of such power it could mimic emotional intelligence. And she accused him of being out of touch! This doll wasn't some dumb piece of plastic that uttered two or three pre-programmed words in an endless loop. It was capable of learning! It was cutting edge.

'Gibberish?' His wife was swollen with rage, face flushed, mouth set in a thin line. She took a step towards him. 'You pig. You disgust me.'

'Well, if I'm so disgusting, why don't you just pack up and leave, huh?'

She laughed, but it was cold and sharp.

'Oh, no,' she said. 'One of us is leaving, but it's not me.'

The voices filtered through to Briony's bedroom, but she paid no attention.

The doll was beautiful. She cradled it in her arms. Daddy would put the batteries in later when he'd stopped talking to Mummy. For now she just admired its perfect skin and hair. She brushed a hand along the doll's cheek, rested a finger against a curling eyelash.

When the doll snapped open its eyes, she froze. The glass orbs beneath the lids were dark and empty. They swivelled, slowly, deliberately, around the bedroom before fixing on the girl's face. The rosebud mouth opened.

'Hello, Briony,' it said.

The eyes were black, almost lifeless, yet something hard glittered in their centres. But the face was so delicate, so innocent.

'Hello,' said Briony. 'You're beautiful.'

A small tongue licked at small lips. It smiled.

'But you aren't,' it said. 'In fact, you're disgusting.

You're a pig.'

The girl's face clouded. She felt tears pricking at her lids.

'You are not nice,' she said through her tears. 'I don't like you. I will tell Daddy to take you back to the shop.'

The doll laughed.

'You don't understand,' it said. 'Oh, one of us will have to leave, Briony. But I can tell you right now it won't be me.'

Revenge

Ben Harmer

Illustration by Heath McKenzie

'NO!' I SCREAMED. 'No, no, no, NO!'

I awoke sweaty and feeling like a drowned, terrified rat. 'Another nightmare,' I thought. 'Why is this happening to me? I've had the same nightmare every night for four weeks in a row.'

As I looked up over my bed, I saw a person kneeling there. He was short and stubby with slick black hair. It was Norm, my old imaginary friend from second grade.

'What—' I yelped as I jumped off the bed.

'Hey, Mick-ey.' He whooped like he hadn't seen me in five years. Come to think of it he hadn't. 'How are you doing my friend?' He paused. 'Living high?' His mood changed into a mean and angry scowl which

looked for retribution. Suddenly, he swung a huge
punch right to my face and I crashed to the ground.
My room got darker and Norm faded.

I awoke sweaty and terrified again, but this time it
was no dream. I was tied up. The room was dark and I
could feel evil in the air. As I widened my eyes, I could
see a blade right in front of me stopping any thoughts
of escape. Then a light flickered on and Norm entered.

'Mike, my friend' he said. 'You must be doing well
ever since you got rid of me. Remember when your
Mummy said that there was no Norm and I was just
your imagination? You believed her, didn't you Mike?'

I finally stuttered 'N-N-Norm? You can't be real.
Y-y-you just can't.'

'Ah, but that's where you're wrong, Mike. You
see, ever since your head has been so stressed, you
haven't had the strength to keep all those bad doors
in your brain locked away. I got out. Along with a lot
of other things you've imagined.'

I was speechless.

Norm smiled.

'Remember the monster we used to hide from —
the one in your wardrobe?' he said. 'Well, let's meet it
again.'

As I looked towards the wardrobe, I saw a filthy green beast, with dribbling fangs and smelled a breath so foul that it would fell any prey it wanted.

'Or the ghost of the closet who chased us?' he added, as a white ghost with disgusting black eyes came to life from behind my curtains. It looked at me and saw right through my soul.

'And remember the dreaded Shadow Man who had four knives?' he continued, and a shadow of a man swooped down from the ceiling.

'Do you see what happens when you try to forget us?' Norm snorted in disgust. 'We will always come back to haunt you.' He laughed like a vampire that has just met his next victim. Then, he disappeared.

My ropes and the blade disappeared. I was untied but I wished I wasn't.

'There's no way I can defeat these things, they can't die. They are just my imagination.'

The green monster, the white ghost and the shadow man were coming closer to feed off me.

'That's it!' I thought as my mind sparked. 'My imagination!'

I rolled up my sleeves and had some serious thoughts.

'Hey, Norm!' I shouted.

'Yes, Mike?' his chuckling voice came from the dark.

'I remember all these things.' I said smartly. 'These things are scary. But I remember other things, too. Like how I found out that the green monster was just my old green jacket hung on the back of my door.' Suddenly the monster turned into that old green jacket and fell to the dark ground.

'Wait! What?' I watched Norm's legs appear.

'And that the ghost,' I continued, 'was just a bed sheet from the laundry closet.' The ghost that had been flying about my head suddenly turned back to a white sheet and settled onto the ground with its green friend.

'No!' Norm growled, as his torso appeared.

'Plus the Shadow Man was really just my cat Timmy's shadow, with his four big claws.'

Then shadow man who had been lurching towards me turned into Timmy, my cat.

'No, you can't do that, Mike. You just can't!' Norm screeched as his head finally appeared and he was a full body.

I knocked Norm flat on his back.

'And you my friend...' I said '...are just a pure figment of my imagination!'

'No, please, Mike, I beg you. You forgot about me. You made me nothing.'

'Norm, YOU ARE NOTHING!' I yelled.

'No, no, no!' Norm shouted as he disappeared for good.

I awoke sweaty once again.

'Are you all right, Mike?' said Mum in her soft, comforting voice. She was standing next to my bed. 'You seemed to be having a nightmare.'

'I'm fine, Mum. I have already gone through the nightmare, but it was nothing... just my imagination.'

Aunt Eda's Piano

Sue Lawson

ZAC DUMPED his school bag on the family room floor. An old baby grand piano crouched in the corner of the room.

'What's that thing doing here already?' he said.

Mum looked up from her magazine. 'Don't start, Zac.'

'I hate piano, especially that piano.'

'I don't care,' snapped Mum. 'Aunt Eda's will clearly states that if you learn one piece on her piano and play it at the eisteddfod, everything she owned is ours. Everything. Her money, jewellery, antiques and the house.'

A shiver ran down Zac's spine. Aunt Eda's brick house crouched on the cliff overlooking Norfolk Bay.

Every time he'd visited, even on warm days, the ocean bubbled and boiled, slapping the cliff with icy spray. The wind screamed up the cliff, stunting the trees in Aunt Eda's garden, making them look like kids frozen while playing.

Inside, Aunt Eda's house was grey and moody. Dust floated in the weak sunlight that filtered through the tiny windows, jars filled with muddy blobs in murky liquid lined the kitchen shelves. Bundles of drying flowers and leaves hung from the ceiling in every room, even the toilet.

And there was always Aunt Eda herself, with her moustache and gnarled walking stick that she poked at Zac at any opportunity.

'I don't want her dump of a house and I don't want to play her stupid piano,' said Zac. 'Why can't Maisie do it? She still has piano lessons.'

'Because Aunt Eda's will named you, not your sister.' Mum slammed her magazine on the coffee table. 'And you may not want her dump, young man, but you're certainly enjoying her money.' Mum looked from the new plasma TV to Zac as she picked up creased music sheets from the coffee table.

'Now, stop whining and play.'

Zac took the sheets. They were dusty and smelt of Aunt Eda. He read the title. '"The Ghost". Hmm…figures.' He slunk to the piano. 'Wish I could practise at Nan's like I used to. Her piano isn't scratched and dented like this one. And her keys aren't yellow and flaky.'

'Aunt Eda's piano is worth a fortune, Zac. And those keys are ivory.'

'Like teeth? Gross!' Zac folded his arms. 'I'm definitely not playing.'

'Fine. I guess I'll take this new stuff back,' said Mum marching across the room to the TV. 'So should we send back your Playstation first? Or your mobile phone and iPod?'

'Okay. But so you know, I hate Aunt Eda even more now she's dead.' Zac thumped a chord.

Pain stabbed his index finger.

'It stabbed me,' he screamed, pulling his hand away. Blood lay on the E key. As he watched, the blood shimmered and disappeared. The key changed from stained and chipped to dazzling white. 'Mum, seriously, it—'

'The TV goes,' yelled Mum.

'All right, but this thing is going to kill me.'

'Get on with it, Zac.'

Zac practised piano every day, and every day he
nicked a finger on the piano's keys. Before his eyes
the blood would shimmer and the key would change
from old and stained to perfect and white. The first
three keys to change were an E, a D and an A.

'This thing is trying to eat me, Mum, I swear,'
said Zac, rummaging through the kitchen drawer for
another bandaid.

Mum thrust her finger at the plans of her dream
home pinned to the kitchen wall. The dream home
she'd build to replace Aunt Eda's house on the cliff
overlooking Norfolk Bay.

So Zac kept playing and bleeding, and after a
while, he was too tired to complain.

A week before the eisteddfod, Zac woke to his mother
shaking him. 'It's after 11,' she said.

'So?' mumbled Zac, his arms and legs as heavy as
an elephant.

'It's your sister's dance recital, remember?'

'Do I have to come?'

'No. You're to stay home and practise piano

instead.' Mum threw back the covers. 'Up and into it. You're fading away lying here.'

Zac could barely pull on his jeans and tee shirt. It was as though they were made of bricks, not cotton.

'Zac, you look terrible,' said Maisie, standing in the kitchen in her leotard and pink tutu.

'He's fine,' snapped Mum, slinging her handbag over her shoulder. 'We'll be back in an hour. Practise hard.' She marched to the back door.

'See you, Zac,' said Maisie, squeezing his hand before skipping after their mother.

Zac yawned and trudged to the piano. This time when he hit the keys, he couldn't pull his hands away. With the sound of a D, an E, an A and a D filling the room, Zac slumped forward, unable to fight the feeling he was being sucked into the piano.

It was late afternoon when Mum walked into the family room. 'Where is that boy?' she said. 'He should still be practising.'

'Hey, he's polished Aunt Eda's piano. It looks like new,' said Maisie. She walked across the room, lifted the piano lid a little, and retrieved Zac's shoe.

'Wonder what that's doing there?' she said.

Clowns

Zoe Boyd

I'M NOT scared of anything;
not the dark or clowns or monsters
Those things are scary
But I'm not scared
Though... Clowns are scary, aren't they?
Their gnashing teeth. Red noses. And dancing eyes
Who wouldn't fear them?
They entrance you. Entertain you. Hate you
And we laugh and clap. Afraid.
Cheering in the near darkness. Popcorn flying.
Swirling red lights. Glittering eyes.
They creep up with gloved hands. Reaching.
You laugh and back away
Shaking your head

'No, I don't want to be eaten, thank you.'
Curly hair, bright clothes.
Stupid shoes.
Happy painted faces on grotesque features
Of course, I'm not scared
They won't hurt me, much.
I'll just wait in the dark;
for the monsters.
Then we'll go to the circus.

Clowns are scared of monsters
you know.

Ute Man

Bernadette Kelly

IT HAD been Adam's idea to follow the bearded man in the blue ute — to find out more about him.

'Don't you think that's his business?' Luke had argued.

'But don't you wonder about him? Just a little? He comes into town every week and never buys anything but cigarettes. What does he live on?' Adam asked.

The boys were hiding behind the community noticeboard outside Sampson's Supermarket. No one knew they were there.

'What's he doing?' asked Luke.

Adam peered around the board then drew back again.

'Can't see him. Hey, Red's selling his BMX,' Luke

said, reading from the notice board.

'That notice is out of date,' said Luke. 'He sold it last holidays.'

'And the Bourke family's got kittens for sale.'

'They always have kittens,' said Luke.

'There's a notice here about those missing hikers,' said Adam.

'That was last summer,' said Luke. 'Did they ever find—'

Adam nudged his friend. 'Shut up. Here he comes.'

The boys hopped on their trail bikes and discreetly tailed the ute until it took off with a roar ten kays from town. They followed the dust wake it left behind as it left the dirt road and followed a path of its own making. So intent were they on catching up with the ute, they nearly missed it, parked in the scrub, partially hidden.

There was no sign of ute man.

'What now?' Luke asked. He looked up at the sky. 'It'll be dark soon. And no one knows where we are.'

Adam grinned then clutched at his own throat as he stumbled backwards. 'OH NO! WE COULD DIE OUT HERE,' he shouted dramatically.

'Shutup idiot! Listen,' Luke said.

The sound of running water was faint in the distance. They followed the sound through the tangled scrub until it led them to a waterfall gushing straight from a sandstone cliff face. A flash of colour caught their attention behind the waterfall, then it was gone. Adam clambered up onto a ledge that ran behind the falling water.

'There's a tunnel.' Adam's voice echoed as he moved deeper into the rock opening.

Luke scrambled upward and followed Adam into a smooth-walled gorge that opened out into a sheltered valley. The opening they'd passed through made a wall around three sides of the valley, while a steep, thickly treed bank protected the land to the west. Amongst the scattered trees were cultivated plots of flourishing herbs and vegetables.

'Incredible,' Adam whispered. 'He lives here! The ute man. And he's totally self-sufficient. Look, there's a cave. I bet he lives in there. Hello?'

Inside the cave, a swag was rolled out on the sandy floor. A fire burning in a shallow pit cast eerie shadows across the rock walls. Eight brightly coloured backpacks were lined up neatly against one wall. Behind the fire was a thick slab of timber, which had been turned into a rough table. A pile of bones lay on an otherwise empty plate.

Hidden in the shadows was a narrow passage. Someone coughed sharply.

'He's here,' whispered Luke.

The boy's shoulders scraped against the walls of the narrow tunnel. Darkness engulfed them. Adam grabbed Luke's shirt and Luke yelped as his foot connected with something hard.

'What is it?' Adam whispered.

'Can't see. I need light,' said Luke.

'Here,' said Adam, groping in his shirt pocket. He flicked open a cigarette lighter.

'A lighter?' asked Luke, turning to look at Adam in the glow of the flame.

'I found it. At school.' Luke shrugged. 'Thought it might come in handy.'

Again, there was a cough. They turned around and the slight flame from the lighter revealed a woman hunkered down in a small cage. Her hair was matted and filthy, and she stared at them through the cage bars with an empty expression.

'What—?' Like gasped.

Adam moved the lighter to the right to discover

more cages, holding another woman, two men and a child. All were filthy.

And then the noise began — a deafening racket of demented, despairing howls.

'What... who are they?' asked Luke.

Adam's eyes met Luke's as he pointed to the backpacks lined up so neatly against the wall.

'Backpacks... You think they're the missing hikers?' said Luke. 'But there were eight of them. And there are only five people here—'

'We have to leave. Now!' said Adam, urgently.

Suddenly a wide beam of torchlight played across the boys. A tall shadowy figure stood blocking the exit.

'Hello, boys,' it said.

No one knew where they were...

Eat Your Words

Janeen Brian

Illustration by Clara Batton Smith

'SERENA! I'VE only got three dollars left!'

The girls paused in the sideshow alley, while Taryn checked her purse again.

'No wonder,' said Serena. 'Four show-bags, five rides, a hot dog, fairy-floss and two games at the shooting gallery.'

'But that's my bus fare home.'

'We can still *look* at things, misery-guts,' Serena grinned. 'Come on! Let's see the baby animals.'

As they passed the doughnut stall, Taryn took a deep, appreciative sniff.

'Go ahead,' chuckled Serena. 'Sniffing's free.'

They swaggered along, laughing and bumping into each other until Taryn cried, 'Hey, look at them!'

In front of a striped tent was a stall displaying

large, coloured gobstoppers wrapped in cellophane.

'Three dollars each,' said the stallholder.

'Three?' said Taryn.

'Special gobstopper.' The woman's almond-eyes glinted. 'Full of words.'

'What do you mean?' Taryn edged closer.

'As you suck, so words appear.'

'On the gobstopper?'

'Right to the very centre. Dozens of words.'

Taryn glanced at Serena. 'I love the sound of that!'

'Money, Taryn,' Serena whispered out the side of her mouth.

'I know.' Taryn tapped her foot. She stared at the gobstopper, then at the ground and back to the gobstopper.

'All the words you'll ever need,' said the woman, leaning in, and smiling with closed lips.

'Okay.' Taryn opened her purse, ignoring Serena's loud grunt behind her.

The clear paper wrapper crackled as Taryn pulled it free. 'Oh, smell it, Serena. Divine.' She stuck the sweet in her mouth and crossed her eyes. 'Tastes divine too!'

'Now you'll have to walk home.'

Taryn removed the gobstopper to check if any words had appeared. 'At least I'll have something to do while I'm walking!'

Serena shook her head. 'You're hopeless.'

Five minutes later Taryn squealed, 'There are words!' She squinted. 'Culprit. Eyewash. Follicle. Gerbil!'

Both girls laughed.

'Such handy, everyday words,' said Serena. 'Hey, I'd better catch my bus. See ya tomorrow.' She hugged Taryn and walked off.

'Mmm,' mumbled Taryn, entranced with the words. By the time she looked up, Serena was fifty metres away. 'Slime-juice!' Taryn shouted cheerily and waved.

For a full second her mouth remained open like a fish.

Had she really said what she thought she'd said? She looked around. There'd been no one nearby. It must've been her. But why? Lucky Serena hadn't heard.

Bewildered, Taryn trudged out of the Show Grounds and turned left along a leafy street, the incident still in her mind. At the traffic lights, she removed the gobstopper from her mouth and checked again for words. The earlier ones had gone but new ones were appearing.

One stood out like a beacon.

The traffic light turned green and the pedestrian buzzer blared but Taryn couldn't move.

The word on the gobstopper was . . . slime-juice!

A car horn honked. She jumped and stumbled across the road. On the other footpath she checked again and shook her head. It was a weird coincidence and it gave her the shudders.

As she turned the next corner, a wild wind sprang up from nowhere. Leaves skittered and Taryn's dark hair flickered across her face.

'A bit blowy,' commented a man, holding onto his hat.

'Immunity,' Taryn replied politely. 'Oozy video.'

The man lowered his brows and hurried on.

Taryn gasped. She felt sick. What was she saying! What was going on?

Then she had a thought. Sugar. That was it. She'd had so much junk food at the show, she must be having a sugar fit. Relieved with this diagnosis, she sighed and hurried on. She'd phone Serena when she got home and they'd both have a good laugh about it.

At the top of her street, Taryn checked the words again. This time they were blurred so she didn't bother to try and work them out. Besides, she'd almost finished the gobstopper and the insides of her cheeks felt crinkly from so much sweetness.

Suddenly she saw a caramel-coloured puppy nosing through the bars of a gate. Taryn knelt and extended her hand.

'Hiccup, you heroic, heated marble,' she murmured, stroking the silky fur.

The little dog gazed at Taryn with bright, dark eyes.

But Taryn sank to the footpath.

Her head spun. The gobstopper fell from her hand. It lay beside her, the words visible even from that distance.

Hiccup. You. Heroic. Heated. Marble.

A cold chill shot up and down her body and her hands fluttered to her mouth. What had the stallholder said? That the gobstopper contained all the words you would ever need.

Slowly the truth of those words dawned on her as she struggled to stand.

Somehow she knew now that the only words she would ever be able to use were those that she'd sucked from the gobstopper.

White-faced and trembling, she opened the back door.

'Hi, darling,' called her mum. 'Did you and Serena have a nice time at the Show? Come and tell me all about it.'

Fear
Lorraine Marwood

FEAR GROWS
first in the dark oblong
beneath night time beds,
spreads to the scratches
behind wardrobe doors,
fogs over
the dressing table mirror
and dances in billows
through every curtain.

It bursts
through the rattly windows
and somersaults into a giant's shadow
until I stop feeding

that fear
cut off the food source
of worry and thought,
then fear
shrinks to a dark triangle
that stains
the carpet with the last ghosting
of night time fright,
waiting for the morning light
to clean it away.

Tooth Fairy

Dianne Touchell

THE TOOTH FAIRY always comes at night when the moon is just on the wane, and its cool surface begins to pit like a molar. The light from this toothy moon is always shy and grey turning shadows a smoky blue and trees into petrified dancers. This was the time. She was sure of it.

She squeezed one fist tight around her tiny treasure. The baby tooth she held had fallen out two weeks ago and she had been waiting for a night just like this to offer it up. She had washed it and polished it. She had scratched away as much of the brownish blood tarnishing the small root as she could. She rested her other hand, palm flat, against the bedroom window. The glass was cold.

Before climbing into bed she dropped the tooth into the glass of water on her bedside table. It drifted to the bottom, finally landing with a barely audible ping. She climbed into bed and turned on her side, pulling the pillow under her chin. The tooth fairy wouldn't come while she was awake. From where she lay she could see her tooth. It looked much larger and rounder sitting in the water. Like a giant's tooth. Like the moon's surface. Like the tooth of a giant who lived on the moon.

She didn't realise she had fallen asleep until she was startled awake. She didn't realise she had been startled until the rapid thumping of her heart began to subside. The room was cool, the last of the risen moon's burnish casting a silver flush over the bed. She rolled over and looked up at the glass of water. At first she thought it was a trick of the light. Or perhaps her eyes had not adjusted from sleep yet. That's when she sat up and peered in the glass, first from the side, then from the top. It was true. The tooth was gone.

A coil of excitement began to turn in her chest until she realised the missing tooth had not been replaced by money. Wasn't that the deal? She was sure she had been told the tooth fairy bought the teeth. There was supposed to be coins in the water and, from what she'd been told, a lot of them! She picked up the glass and examined the bottom just in case. No tooth, no money. She pushed the glass back onto her bedside table with enough force to splash water over the side and felt the first bubbles of fury begin to rise.

'I need more.'

It was so quiet at first she wasn't sure she had heard it at all. It was less, and more, than a whisper. It was a creaking breath, a small scratch in the cool air. She sat back on her haunches pressing herself against the wall. Her fingers curled around the edge of the pillow beneath her as she stared into the half light. All of her familiar things suddenly seemed so unfamiliar. Her eyes were wide and dry. She blinked hard and licked her lips and felt sweat prickling her scalp.

'I need more.'

This time the words chinked like staccato and were attended by a slow movement at the foot of her bed. Her skin jumped into gooseflesh as a large shadow unfurled itself. It seemed to come from nothing, or from the nothingness beyond the sluice of light still cast by the moon. Dread dropped into her stomach like a stone in a pond and she found she couldn't speak, couldn't call out. The figure rose into the air, dark on dark, and then began to crawl toward her. She could feel its weight on the bed, hear the springs singing. She opened her mouth to scream, only to feel a hand clamp around her jaw. In shock she swallowed the scream in a swell of air and accidentally burped instead.

'You have beautiful teeth.'

Its breath was sweet smelling and cool as the air. A gentle warmth began in her chin and spread all the way to her gums. She was being lifted. She felt herself rising slowly from the bed and wondered, just for a moment, if she would bump her head on the ceiling. It was like being in water and waiting to break the surface. There was no panic. There was simply the knowledge that she was about to find out just what the fairies used human teeth for.

By morning she was far away. Her room was as she had left it except for a glass on the bedside table, sitting in a pool of water, filled to the brim with gold coins.

Mama Told Me

Melissa Keil

MAMA TOLD me never to go near the water.

But Mama told me lots of things that made no sense. Like, never take sweets from strangers, and never play in the street, and never use a knife in the toaster. Mama had too many rules to follow. Anyway, I rode my bike on the street loads of times when she wasn't looking, and nothing bad ever happened to me.

The pond in Mrs McGreevy's garden was almost hidden behind the row of trees that Mama had planted along our fence. But if I climbed on my swing-set and stood high on my toes, I could sometimes see the green-blue water sparkling through the branches, could just make out the stone angels that sat, smiling, on the top of the cracked fountain.

Sometimes when I slept, I dreamt about chocolates, or spiders, or the new bike I wanted for my birthday. Lots of times I dreamt about the water.

One night the dream woke me.

My head was still fuzzy with sleep, and I thought for a second that Mama was calling me. I could hear my name, softly, over and over and over again. The voice drifted into my bedroom, sweet and cheerful. I needed to see who owned that voice.

It came from the garden, from behind Mrs McGreevy's tall fence. Her gates were always held closed with a big, brass lock, only this time, there was no lock. As I touched them, shivering in my pajamas, the gates swung open.

In the distance, the water shimmered. I walked closer to the pond, the voice still singing my name.

The stone angels smiled down at me.

I dipped my littlest finger in the water, swirling it through the stars twinkling on the surface, watching them flicker from tiny dots to fuzzy balls of light.

The voice was softer now, almost too soft to hear, but I listened and listened, and I heard it call my name again.

I reached into the water.

And something reached back for me.

It caressed my hand with velvety fingers that felt like the soft marshmallows Mama kept in a box near her bed. It stroked the skin around my wrist, wrapping gently around my arm.

And then it pulled me under.

I tried to reach up, tried to grab hold of the angels. But the angels weren't smiling any more. They screamed at me, their faces twisted, tiny teeth flashing through howling mouths.

I could see the water above me; only, it didn't look like water anymore. It swirled and spun and twisted, fingers of mist reaching towards me, poking in my eyes and my ears, and I think I screamed but my mouth filled with fog and I couldn't make a sound.

The voice laughed and laughed and laughed.

And then I was gone.

Sometimes when the wind blows, I can still hear Mama calling me.

I wonder what she would say if she could see me now.

Probably,

'I told you so.'

Haunted

Katherine Battersby

I'LL NEVER forget that day. Staring down at the concrete, the sun strangely cool on the back of my neck.

Thick dark skid-marks careened across the road and jumped the footpath, as if scrawled by an unsteady hand. The sight sent a speckle of goose bumps up my bare arms. A vague memory of last night's dream surfaced in my mind. The details were sketchy, but there'd been some kind of car crash. It was too strange to be a coincidence. I wondered if there'd really been an accident and the sounds had filtered into my dreams.

I shivered then and had that sudden sense of being watched. My eyes were pulled from the concrete to find a small gangly girl across the street. She wore a flimsy white dress, her blonde hair swirling eerily around her face. She was deathly pale. I'm not easily spooked, but I'm ashamed to say I backed towards my house and hurried inside. A strange beginning to an even stranger day.

My mind was still jumping around like a spark, so I tried watching TV. Monster-Truck-Mayhem had already started, a show Dad got me hooked on. It usually helped me unwind after an afternoon of footy training, but not this day. The truck's tyres left thick ridges in the mud, a constant reminder of the strange skid marks outside. Rubbing my face roughly, I went to get up, but the morning paper caught my eye. It perched on the coffee table, folded to reveal a single bold headline, as if wanting me to read it.

'Fatal Mistake' read the article, telling in its detached tone the story of a car that had veered off the road, trying to avoid an animal. A child had been hit and killed, and although they weren't releasing any names, they mentioned my suburb.

Downstairs, I found Dad in his office.

'You hear anything last night?' I asked. 'Like car tyres? Screeching?'

My voice echoed off the walls. But Dad didn't answer. He stared at his drawing desk, brow furrowed and eyes distant. I knew he had a big design project on at work, meaning he needed lots of 'creative space', so I left him alone.

My mind stuck on the accident, I wandered to the kitchen and scanned the sagging shelves, but my stomach wasn't speaking to me that day. A shiver crackled up my spine and I glanced out the front window. The girl now stood outside my house, staring down at the footpath. As I watched, she looked up, our eyes locking. A fist of ice clenched my heart as I realised who she was. She was the kid from the accident. She was a ghost.

Ignoring the alarm bells ringing in my ears, I stumbled outside. She now stood across the road against a row of hedges, still staring at me. But when I blinked, she was gone. I sprinted across the road, sneakers barely touching the hot bitumen. At the hedges I glimpsed a flicker of white disappear into the parklands. Every instinct told me to flee, but instead I took chase.

As I hurtled through the trees, the whisper of white just ahead, my mind raced. Who was this ghost and what did she want? I knew these parks well, but couldn't tell where she was leading me. She made no noise as she ran, the air broken only by my breath, punching out of me with each step.

Racing around the corner, I skidded to a halt. The skeleton of a playground sprawled in an unfamiliar clearing. Paint flaked from the crooked climbing frame, the slide cracked and fallen. Only one swing remained, creaking in the non-existent breeze.

Instinct drew me to the concrete tunnel, formed from an old council drain. Hands clenched so tightly my nails should've drawn blood, I ducked under the concrete lip and folded myself into the darkness. Inside, I found the ghost.

Her eyes darted towards me, wide and wild. Her hands groped blindly behind her, finding only the stained wall.

'Why are you haunting me?' she said.

'Haunting?' I barked, my voice tightened by fear.

'It wasn't my fault,' she yelped. 'I was out looking for Mittens. It was so dark. She was in the middle of the road. I tried to call her away, but the car came around the corner,' she pleaded. 'It all happened so fast. I didn't know you were there...'

My mind reeled as everything came together in frightening clarity: the way hunger no longer called to me; Dad, distant and unresponsive; the skid marks outside my house; the strange dream.

It was no dream.

And the girl wasn't pale because she was a ghost. She was pale because she was looking at one.

Destiny Meets Girl

Shirley Marr

LISTEN UP children; do what your parents say or else your destiny might catch up with you. I know because it happened to me.

It was a perfect summer's day. Too perfect for it to be the first day back at school. I was upstairs in my bedroom, dawdling. I pulled on my school shirt, really slowly.

I pulled on my checked skirt, even more slowly.

I stared at the socks and shiny black Mary Janes lying on the floor — shackles for my feet that longed to be outside, barefoot.

'What is taking so long?' My mother's voice drifted up from downstairs.

'Almost ready!' I shouted back.

I sighed and stared at my school bag that looked too heavy to carry.

'Stop dawdling!' Mum called again. 'Remember, little girls who don't listen to their mothers will meet with their destiny!'

'Yeah, yeah,' I thought, annoyed she had called me a little girl.

'I'm not joking! I've got your lunch and the car ready — neither will be waiting around for the next twenty years!'

I wish Mum knew what it was like going to school. I sighed once again, went to the wardrobe and pulled open the door.

Standing inside my wardrobe was a woman in a black dress.

My eyes widened in horror and my mouth popped open. The air around me suddenly turned cold and prickly. I slammed the door shut.

Without another complaint, I pulled on my socks and my shoes, grabbed my backpack and tore down the stairs.

'Well, finally,' said Mum.

I grabbed my lunch and ran all the way to the car. I strapped on the seat belt and listened to the thump

thump of my racing heart as Mum took forever to come out. I'd never wanted to get to school so badly. My eyes wandered up the face of the house to my bedroom window. It stared back at me like an eye. I shuddered and covered my face.

That night after school, I did all my homework without complaining just so I could stay downstairs where Mum and the lights were. I didn't want to go upstairs to my room. Finally, though, I had no choice, but to go back up and change into my pyjamas. I approached the wardrobe door. The wardrobe door stared back at me. I walked a little closer. The door stared at me a little closer.

Don't give Mum another chance to call you a little girl; don't give Mum another chance to call you a little girl I repeated to myself over and over.

My shaking hand reached out for the handle. I thought I saw the handle turn itself a little, but it must have been my imagination. I grabbed hold of the handle and wrenched the door open.

There was nothing. Just my rack of clothes. Shoes underneath. Winter woollies packed up on the top shelf. I quickly grabbed the first pair of pyjamas I saw and slammed the door shut.

That night in the dark, the door seemed to glow by itself. Every time I felt myself drift into sleep, my eyes would suddenly fly open, ready to see the woman in the black dress creep out of the wardrobe. Into the darkness and toward me.

I was the perfect daughter and student after that 'wardrobe incident'. I got along better with Mum and spent more time with her instead of staying locked up in my room like I used to. I was happier at school because I spent more time studying downstairs at home. I did better in my subjects. I didn't tell a single soul about why I had changed.

Time passed and I grew from a child to a teen and then finally to an adult. I never saw the woman in my wardrobe again. I finally put it down to an overactive child's imagination. Maybe secretly, I had wanted something to shock me into being disciplined.

One day, back at my mother's house, I went to my old bedroom looking for old memories. I was immediately drawn to my wardrobe and — shaking my head and laughing — I pulled the door open.

Standing inside the wardrobe was a little girl. She was wearing a school shirt and checked skirt, but no socks or shoes. Her eyes widened in horror and her mouth popped open. She slammed the door shut on me.

The air suddenly turned cold and my skin started to prickle. I looked down at my black dress and my mother's words rang in my ears.

Remember, little girls who don't listen to their mothers will meet with their destiny.

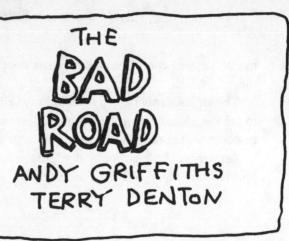

THE BAD ROAD

ANDY GRIFFITHS
TERRY DENTON

Tap, Tap, Tapping at the Window

Laura Bahdus-Wilson

JAMES

WHOOOOEEEEEE.

The wind whistled around the house, cold and
biting like a message from the grave. James couldn't
sleep. The swaying branches outside kept tapping
at his window. He peered timidly out the window.
The full moon cast long dark shadows across his
room... shadows like bony claws, curled with evil rage.

Didn't zombies come out during full moons?

No, wait, that was werewolves.

The moonlight highlighted the horror comic on
his bedside table. James turned the comic over so
he couldn't see the cover then dived back under the
doona. He rolled over to face the wall, shut his eyes
and willed himself to fall asleep. Then, as he started

to drift off, he heard a tap, tap, tapping at his window. TAP, TAP, TAP.

James's eyes flicked open. Surely that was just branches... although... it did sound a little different this time. More like the skeletal knuckles of a decayed body trying to break through the glass.

TAP, TAP, TAP.

There it was again... and then... silence.

James closed his eyes and tried to think of other things like riding his bike and playing cricket.

TAP, TAP, TAP... CREEEAAAAK. CRASH.

Heart pounding heavily, James sat up and swung around to face the window. No one was there. But the window was wide open, and gusts of wind swirled through his room. Loose sheets of paper blew off his desk and scattered across the floor. He could have sworn he saw movement in the darkness.

James leapt out of bed and shut the window. It was only the wind, he kept telling himself. Back under the covers, he waited for his heart to stop racing. His watch told him it was midnight. Wasn't midnight when the dead rose from their graves and haunted the deserted streets?

SCRATCH, SCRATCH, SCRATCH.

What was that?

James's stomach clenched in fear. He tried desperately to ignore the terrible thoughts in his head.

ZZZZZzzzzzzzzzzzz.

He couldn't have imagined that... could he?

James pulled the doona over his head to shut out the sound. Perhaps if the zombie/ghost/werewolf that was in his room couldn't see him, he'd be safe.

Shuffle, Shuffle, Shuffle.

Pitter Patter.

SCRATCH, SCRATCH, SCRATCH.

His eyes wide open, James stared at the darkness under the doona. Logic told him that hiding wouldn't help. Whatever it was that lurked in his room had to be faced and conquered. His cricket bat was under the bed; maybe he could use that as a weapon.

It was now or never.

James flung the doona off, somersaulted out of bed and, rigid with fear, stood horrified. A ghost glided across his room, and then the same terrifying petrifying ghost turned and headed his way.

James couldn't be brave. He didn't have time to reach for his bat. He opened his mouth and screamed until his voice gave out.

BORIS

Boris was trying to sleep but the cold wind kept churning through his rickety kennel. He thought about how warm it would be inside the house, and wondered again why he was the only one sent outside to sleep. Boris crawled out of his kennel and padded around to the front of the house. He knew he could count on James to let him sneak inside for the night.

Moonlight painting his black coat silver, Boris got up on his hind legs and scratched at James's window with his front paws.

TAP, TAP, TAP.

No response. He pressed his muzzle against the glass and saw that James looked fast asleep.

TAP, TAP, TAP.

TAP, TAP, TAP.

CREEEAAAAK. CRASH.

What luck! The window hadn't been shut properly.

Boris jumped through the open window and scurried under the bed. It was warmer there... and probably better to be hidden in case anyone else from the family came in.

SCRATCH, SCRATCH, SCRATCH.

He always enjoyed a good scratch before curling

137

up. The carpet under the bed was so warm and soft that it wasn't long before he fell fast asleep.

ZZZZZzzzzzzzzzzz.

Boris woke when James moved around in the bed above. He wondered if he should come out and say hello. On the other hand, it really was nice and warm under the bed.

Although, actually now... it was getting a bit stuffy.

Shuffle, shuffle, shuffle.

Pitter Patter.

SCRATCH, SCRATCH, SCRATCH.

Boris crawled out from under the bed and snuggled into a pile of dirty clothes he found in one corner of the bedroom. He loved the way James's clothes smelled like soap and pencils.

Oh wait... he'd forgotten to go over and say hello.

Boris stood up, draped in a white T-shirt from the pile of clothes, and ambled over to the bed.

Oh good... James was already awake...

ARGHHHHHHHHHHHHHHHH.......

What is Mine

Holly Harper

HELENA STOOD before the crypt that had haunted
her dreams for the past few nights. She fought to
stay calm, lifting the ragdoll in her hands up to the
moonlight and stroking her long black hair.

'Almost there, Lizzie.'

The doll didn't answer. She just kept grinning her
crooked, stitched-on smile. Helena took a deep breath
and pushed open the crypt door.

Helena knew now that funerals were boring events.
It wasn't even like she really knew her Great Uncle
Ron, so when nobody was looking, she'd snuck away.
She wound her way through the tombstones doubting
anyone would miss her, least of all Great Uncle Ron.

As she explored the gravestones, a black stone crypt caught her eye. She felt as though somebody — or something — in there was watching her. Helena shivered and was about to turn away when something made her glance down. An old rag doll lay in the crack of the doorway, dirty and forgotten.

Helena reached down to pick it up, its sawdust-filled arms flopping at its sides. She brushed back its long black hair to reveal a crooked smile. There was something about the doll that made her want to take it. Helena knew she shouldn't take something from a grave. She knew she was too old to be playing with dolls, too, but it just seemed too lonely to leave behind.

'I'll call you Lizzie,' she told the doll, who just smiled back.

Helena glanced around to make sure nobody was looking and slipped Lizzie in her pocket. Then she left to rejoin the funeral.

Helena clutched Lizzie as she went to sleep that night, tucking her down low so nobody could see her. She knew it was silly, but she just couldn't shake the idea that Lizzie had been alone for so long and now she'd finally found a friend to comfort her.

When she did fall asleep, Helena dreamt of the crypt. She watched, unable to move as she pushed open the heavy door. Her heart leapt as she saw somebody in the shadows, a girl a few years younger than herself. She looked like she'd been crying. Helena was about to reach out to comfort her when the girl turned towards her, staring with dull, lifeless eyes.

'You have what is mine,' she moaned, her voice heavy with sorrow.

Helena glanced down at the dream-Lizzie in her hand.

'This doll?' she asked.

The ghost girl's eyes welled up with tears. 'Bring her back,' she whispered.

Helena woke suddenly, the girl's sadness still strong within her. She clutched Lizzie tighter, not wanting to give her back.

Helena had the dream three more times before she realised she had no choice. She knew what she must do.

As Helena pushed open the crypt door she expected to see the shadowy girl crouched in a corner, but the crypt was empty. She wondered if she'd let

her imagination get to her, but she couldn't deny
that the dreams were a warning. Stepping inside the
dusty vault, Helena took Lizzie out and placed her on
the ground, relieved it was done. But as she turned to
leave she saw a figure blocking her way. Helena froze
in terror.

'You've come back,' said the girl, her voice echoing
around the small crypt. 'And you've brought what is
mine.' The girl glanced at Helena, her eyes dark and
soulful. 'I've been alone for so many years. But that's
all changed now.' The girl smiled a crooked smile.

Helena's heart leapt as she recognised too late the
familiar grin.

'The one who trapped me here a hundred years
ago told me there was only one way out — to find
another to take my place.'

Helena felt dizzy, as if the world was spinning.

'She told me this as she took my place, and the
one before her took her place, and so on for hundreds
of years before. And now I'm taking what is mine.'

Helena tried to move but she couldn't feel her
arms and legs. Her eyes flicked to her side and she
caught sight of her arms. Her flesh and bones were
gone, replaced by rags and sawdust.

She tried to scream but no sound came out.

'You might get lucky,' said the girl who now towered over her, smiling her crooked smile.

'I was here for a hundred years before you picked me up, but the one who trapped me was only here for twenty. You just have to wait. Wait until somebody finds you. Then you can take back what's yours.'

She turned and left, shutting the crypt door and blocking out the moonlight. Helena's tiny body lay there in the darkness, smiling her stitched-on smile, waiting for someone to come.

The Chamber of Horrors

Michael Panckridge

Illustration by Jared Parkinson

A GROUP of school students shuffled slowly towards the exit.

'This place is so creepy,' Jennifer whispered. 'It even smells awful. I can't wait to get outside.'

'Same,' Ben said, secretly relieved he wasn't the only one spooked by the terrified and bloody stares surrounding them.

'Oh come on, what's wrong with you? It's no big deal.' Steve stood mesmerised by a corpse stretched to almost eight foot by a frightening device with handles — the label beneath said it was a rack.

Ben followed Jennifer towards the exit.

'Wait!' said Steve.

Ben turned then groaned. He'd seen that look before. 'Steve?'

'I'm going to spend the night here in the Chamber of Horrors. The school mag article will be fab. Cover for me, okay? Tell Jan for me, would you?'

'Steve, don't be—'

But Steve had already vanished, slipping quietly beneath an old tarpaulin near a display featuring a dockworker who had taken the lives of eleven sailors.

'Time to move on,' a guard said, hustling out the last few visitors.

Lying still beneath the tarp, Steve listened to the voices slowly fade. A door slammed shut. Silence. He waited a few minutes before pushing aside the heavy material and peering out. The Chamber glowed a dull red. He got to his feet and looked around, suddenly feeling very alone.

'Okay, maybe not a good idea,' he muttered, rushing for the exit. 'Hello? Can someone let me out!' he called, thumping the door.

'Welcome, brave person, to the Chamber of Horrors,' a deep voice boomed. Steve spun around, a look of sheer terror on his face.

'Who's that? Where are you?'

'Sit back and enjoy the show.'

It was the automated voice from before. The one

that he'd heard when he'd first entered the building with the school group.

Steve stumbled back, bumping into a blood-spattered zombie. The waxwork model fell to the floor. Steve jumped back.

'Oh yuck!' Steve gasped. Its head had detached from its body and was rolling across the floor.

Steve scrabbled over to the rear wall and slumped to the floor. Minutes ticked by. Someone's sure to be here in a moment, he thought, reaching into his bag to take out his notebook and pen.

'I'm in the Chamber of Horrors. It's creepy, but it's not real. The place is full of wax models of famous criminals and various other spooky beings like vampires and zombies, as well as disfigured and deformed people. Above me there's a half-decayed body hanging in an iron cage. Next to him are five heads, each one lying on a bed of straw in a metal bin. In front of me stands Kenny, the 'Slaughterhouse Slasher', the sailor who committed those murders down at the dockyards. He has a knife in his hand. Even though he's made out of wax and can't hurt me, it looks like he's staring at me.'

Steve looked up. He felt a shiver under the evil

glare of Kenny's glassy gaze. The silence pressed in. Steve leant back and closed his eyes.

'C'mon, Ben,' he whispered.

Steve opened his eyes to see a flicker of movement and suddenly he was wide awake. He breathed in sharply. Kenny the sailor was now sporting a smile as he slowly moved towards Steve.

'H…help!' Steve shrieked, suddenly paralysed. 'No…no…please!' he cried, as the wax model moved closer. Slowly it raised its arm. A small knife glinted red in the lights of the Chamber.

'Welcome, brave person, to the Chamber of Horrors,' Kenny said, grinning a toothless, lopsided smile. Drops of wax oozed like perspiration from his face.

'This isn't the first time someone's pulled a prank like this. Let's hope your friend hasn't messed with any of the exhibits,' the guard said, unlocking the door.

Ben and Jennifer rushed into the Chamber as the overhead lights blinked on. Apart from the headless model lying on the floor, nothing was out of place.

'Steve?' shouted Ben, looking around.

There was no reply.

'Steve, you idiot, come—'

'There he is,' said Jennifer, pointing. 'Steve?'

'Fallen asleep. He must have nerves of steel,' the guard chuckled, picking up Steve's notebook. 'Come on, mate. Time to go home. Hey!' He squatted by Steve, giving the boy a gentle shake.

But Steve didn't wake.

Jennifer screamed.

'Welcome, brave person, to the Chamber of Horrors,' boomed the automated voice.

The House

Joshua Kopp

KNIVES WERE hurled at her from behind. She ducked quickly to avoid them, but one nicked her shoulder. The house was alive, fire streamed out of holes in the floor and walls, her hair was singed. There was a massive bang as the roof behind her began to collapse as she ran out the door.

She had got what she came for, and was going to get out alive.

She thought of her new life ahead, filled with riches — reward for the book she had risked her life to get. She didn't even know why it was so special, nor did she care.

Still running, she tripped over the root of an ancient tree.

A root. She was sure.

As she rose to her feet, the 'root' grasped her ankle, wrenching it. She let loose a cry, but it was too late.

The house had her. More of the 'roots' — more like hands really — emerged from the soil around her, and dragged her back into the destroyed house. Her blood turned to ice. She knew the end was upon her and ceased her struggle, coldly resigned to the fate that awaited her. She closed her eyes. As the last shreds of consciousness slipped away she surrendered to the welcome embrace of oblivion, the book still clutched in her hands. She had failed, as had many others, to escape the house.

Shadows danced along the walls, with no source, barely recognisable except that they were darker than the surrounding gloom. Echoes from... somewhere. Sitting up, she struggled to regain her thoughts. Dried blood caked her face and clothes. She tried to sit up. She felt nothing.

And then it came. A strong urge to go out and feed. On something alive. She wanted it to fight back, to struggle. Why did she want this? She had never been a violent person.

She knew exactly where she was.

She knew where she had to go.

She knew she had to feed.

She didn't know she wasn't breathing.

At the End
of the Street

Jackie Hosking

THERE'S A spooky house at the end of the street
With a creaky gate and a rusted seat
A twisted tree with one dead leaf
And an old black cat and a bag of grief

Late one night on the 3rd of June
Sally and me in the light of the moon
Crept to the house all spooky and still
And rested our chins on the window sill

There inside on the rocking chair
Rocked Mrs Mac with silver hair
Back and forth she creaked and groaned
As the twisted tree and the old gate moaned

Sally and me could only stare
At the spooky woman with the silver hair
Our throats were tight and eyes were wide
As we peered at the woman on the rocker inside

Just then as the moon went dark with a cloud
A noise from inside that was scary and loud
A crash and a thud and a wail and a scream
Then a voice like a sound
      that you'd hear in a dream

And the voice said, 'Who's that lurking outside?'
And we both ducked down in the bushes to hide
Then the voice said, 'Don't be afraid my dears.
Come inside and forget your fears.'

On rusted hinges the front door scraped
And beckoned us in though we tried to escape
But our legs couldn't run
      and our mouths couldn't yell
And our feet crept like they were under a spell

They walked through the door cause they hadn't
    a choice
Getting closer and closer to the old woman's voice
And Sally and me held hands super tight
On the 3rd of June in the full moon's light

We stood in the door of the room with the chair
Rocking old Mrs Mac with the long silver hair
Her eyes sunk deep in a skull-shaped head
And we screamed as we ran
    from the house of the dead

The Mountain

Tali Lavi

THERE'S A hush over the mountain. There always is the day after someone dies. That's what Elsa tells me. She's lived here all her life. If I hadn't met her last week I wouldn't have realised that things are different today. But they are.

Elsa calls the tourists 'mummies' because she says they look like futuristic mummies wrapped up in their high-tech gear.

'You're not the same, Lou,' Elsa reassures me. 'We call it Alp Fever. The moment they come here they lose all sense of reason. You can almost see them dare each other to take on runs that are too difficult or to go off the tracks completely. There are reasons why the tracks exist. They should be stripped of their fluorescent parkas and sent home. The guys get it the worst.'

She's right. Yesterday it was a guy. Not much older than me. He thought he was being cool by taking a jump that wasn't really a jump. But he wasn't. Being cool that is. He was just being stupid.

It's cold today but the sun is out. After two weeks with my friends, I'm going out solo. Sometimes it's better to be by yourself. After hearing the news, I don't want to be surrounded by the group's chatter and laughter as if nothing has happened.

It really is amazing out here. So quiet. The only sound I hear is the whoosh of my skis or those of passing skiers. But then, something changes inside my ears and I can hear the rustle of the wind through the pines, distant bird calls, even the occasional thud of snow clumps falling from overhanging branches. I sit down on a nearby fallen tree stump and enter this secret world of sound.

After a while, I can't help but think of the guy who died. Maybe it happened somewhere close by. The small hairs on my arms all stand up, and there's a sick feeling in my stomach.

To distract myself I get out my thermos and the Harry Potter book I'm in the middle of. Just one chapter and then I'll keep going. The air seems icier than before but the hot chocolate warms me. Soon enough I'm engrossed in the chapter — the bit where Harry is about to die, evil is threatening to triumph, and then Sirius turns up. Sad, wonderful Sirius! I exhale in relief, turn the page and then snow starts to fall.

I look around me and it has become dark. The wind has picked up. It's as if the dark presence of Voldemort has made its way to Interlaken. The clouds sit like a mass of dark grey hounds ready to turn themselves loose and by the time I get myself together, they do, letting out packs of heavy snow that are vicious in their attack. There is no hiding from these... I don't know what to call them, there is nothing delicate, fragile or snowflakey about them. I reach for my goggles and search for the path.

But it's gone and I don't know which way to turn. Every move is a battle but there's no choice. I push ahead but my body has started to shake with the cold and the world has become a snowdome of whirling, inescapable white. The sky, ground and trees have disappeared. I feel as if I'm being forced underwater in a freezing lake, my vision blurs.

I think of what Elsa would do. Though of course

she wouldn't be here in the first place and she definitely wouldn't be stupid enough to get caught out in the storm.

It's no use. I almost sit down and give up, paralysed by this white prison, but then I feel someone next to me. Through the gale and the shriek of the wind, the person pulls on my jacket and he or she — I can't see clearly — motions to me as if to say, 'It's alright. Come with me, I'll take you back to safety.'

I ski alongside the mysterious person until they stop and point to the ground. What can they mean? Trying to concentrate through the whirl, suddenly I can see tracks under trees not yet covered by snow. I turn to my guide but he has gone.

Beginning to cry with relief, I ski quickly following the marks on the ground before they've disappeared and I am lost for good.

What I don't realise is it's his tracks.

The guy who took the jump yesterday.

The jump not to be taken.

I don't realise this until I pick up speed and fall.

Over the edge and into oblivion.

The Hunt

Heather Gallagher

THERE WAS another massacre last night. Blood and flesh were strewn across the backyard.

As I padded across the dewy grass, something stuck to my left moccasin. Something, which until a few short hours ago, had been one of my girls. Cornflakes heaved in my stomach. I swallowed the bile and crossed to the coop to investigate.

My latest brood had consisted of Ginger, Mrs Brown and, okay I admit it, the stupid one, Harriet. They'd been beautiful, brown birds who trusted me. Who had stretched their feathered necks through their chicken wire enclosure when they heard me coming. And who, every day, provided three fresh eggs. They'd lasted eight weeks.

The chooks before had lasted three months.

The ones before that, only one.

The pen was surrounded with chicken wire and I'd shut the gate. Inside the pen was a wooden coop and the girls were shut in by a door with a latch. I swear some wily fox had figured out how to push the latch across.

I'd just begun burying what remained of the hens when I heard a fluttering above me. Harriet!

She'd escaped. And was now pacing the deck of the tree house. I raced up the ladder and took her in my arms. I was rubbing my cheek against her downy back when I heard a scuffling on the fence which could mean only one thing: our neighbour, Mr Reynard.

'G'day Markus,' he said, leaning a fat, white arm on the fence.

'Hi,' I said, barely glancing up.

'How're the girls?'

I looked up at him quickly. Was I dreaming or had he run his tongue over his upper-lip, flicking at his reddish moustache?

'All except this one — gone,' I told him flatly. 'Another fox. Last night.'

Harriet started clucking loudly.

It was her alarm cluck.

'Hmm.' He stroked his auburn whiskers with flabby fingers. 'You know what they say — cunning as a fox and all that.'

A bizarre thought entered my head and I pushed it out. The trauma of the bloodbath was playing havoc with my mind.

We never saw Mr Reynard much — he kept to himself. But every time I lost some hens he seemed to rear his ugly head, scenting the fresh kill.

'I've got to get ready for school,' I said, tucking Harriet under one arm and climbing down. 'See ya.'

At lunchtime, I went to the library and looked up animal trapping on the Net. If a fox could catch my chooks, I would catch a fox. Traps were about 50 bucks a pop, way out of my price range.

That night, I was bathing my baby brother, Jack, when inspiration struck. The baby bath! Propped up with a stick, bacon underneath, it might just work.

Friday night, I told Mum and Dad I wanted to camp out in the tree house. I used my Grandpa's night vision goggles to keep watch.

At midnight, I awoke with a start. A scuffling noise came from the coop. I scrambled down the ladder flashing my torch through the chicken wire. A blur of orange whizzed past, escaping through a hole in the fence.

I scooted back up the ladder and shone my torch into Mr Reynard's yard. Nothing.

Saturday night, I tried the same routine, chewing on jelly beans to stay awake.

At 5.00 a.m. I turned the goggles back to the hole in the fence. And that's when I saw it. A twitchy brown nose, followed by a pointy muzzle, and a sleek orange body. The fox approached the baby bath, cautiously, sniffing around the edge, trying to pull the meat out.

I inched my way down the ladder.

I'd just reached the coop gate when the fox dived under the bath, devouring the bacon. Twenty pieces of organic free-range — cooked.

Its tail swished in satisfaction, dislodging the stick. The bath fell.

I lunged at the bath, pinning it down. The fox went crazy, pawing at the edges, as I made myself comfortable on top of the bath.

I reached into my pocket for my mobile and called the RSPCA.

The massacres had stopped. I bought some friends for Harriet and visited the girls every morning to check for eggs. Three months later a young woman with red spiky hair knocked at our door.

'Hi,' she said, 'I'm Liza. I'm looking for Gerard Reynard, my uncle. He lives next door. At least, I thought he did. The house looks kind of deserted.'

'Um, yeah,' I said. I hadn't thought of Mr Reynard for ages. Suddenly, I felt ill. 'Sorry, we haven't seen Mr Reynard for... months.'

'Oh,' she paused and sniffed the air.

I was expecting her to be upset or say she'd call the police. But she just sniffed the air again, and looked at me curiously.

'Tell me,' she said, licking her lips. 'Do you keep chickens?'

As a Howl Echoed Throughout the Woods

Kelsey Murphy
Illustration by Matthew Shires

BILLY LOVED camp.

The canoeing, the cabins, staying up late and the *No Parents Allowed* sign. He thought of camp as a heavenly resort because he loved everything about it. That is, until the night of the camp fire stories...

'It was the seventh night of camp,' the camp supervisor began in an eerie voice, 'when the full moon had risen high in the night sky, and the stars were not visible. Some say they were hiding from something. Others didn't live to give their opinion. I don't know about any of that, but what I do know is that there was something mighty strange going on that night.' He paused for effect, looked at the frightened faces and continued talking. 'Something was in those woods that night, and it was waiting until the right moment.'

'The r-r-right moment for w-w-what?' whispered a small girl.

'The right moment to deal with unwanted visitors.'

Billy felt worried. 'I would never visit that — thing's — place.'

The supervisor just shook his head and looked Billy straight in the eye. 'We can't escape, my boy, all this land is its home.'

The campers gaped at their supervisor.

'W-w-what did the monster l-l-look like?' asked a teenage boy.

'The monster's appearance has never been confirmed because anyone who has seen the creature has not lived to tell the tale.' The supervisor paused. 'Some say the creature had mutated into a horrendous being after living in the woods for decades.'

The brave, happy campers who set out that day had become a terrified group of nail biters.

'H-h-how can we know when the monster is coming a-a-after us?' This time it was Billy asking. He had made a mental note that if he survived he would never come back to camp again.

'There is only one way to know when the monster is approaching. The wind will blow the camp fire out, there will be a rustle in the bushes and you will hear a howl echoing throughout the woods.'

Billy jumped up from the log he was sitting on. 'That's it I'm getting out of here!'

The camp supervisor grabbed Billy. 'Don't worry, mate,' he said. 'It's only a story.'

Then the wind blew the camp fire out and there was a rustle in the bushes, as a howl echoed throughout the woods.

The Door

James Roy

AT THE bottom end of our new library, down past
the seniors' study room and through the periodicals
section, is a door. It's a simple door, painted a kind
of turquoise, which I'm told is somewhere between
green and blue. Not quite one or the other.

This seems appropriate, being not quite one thing
and not quite another. Portals between worlds need to
be like that, I think. Partly here, partly there, but not
entirely in either.

I've never been through that door. Neither have
my friends. There was talk, once, about a couple of
grade eight girls knocking quietly, before trying the
handle. It was unlocked, and the door swung open.
They went in. Then they hurried out. They didn't like

to talk about what they'd seen. One of those girls left our school a week or two later. I don't know if the two events were connected.

Sometimes Miss Develin — the ancient librarian's assistant who makes most of the threats against students — warns us about the Door. Or, to be more accurate, she warns us about what will happen to us if we break certain library rules. And those consequences often feature the Door.

'Were you girls downloading songs onto those computers?'

'No, Ms Develin.'

'It's Miss Develin. I am not married, I never was married, and I doubt that I ever will be, now.'

She emphasises the 'now' as if her enduring spinsterhood can be attributed to one cause — us, the students who seem hell-bent on defying her clearly printed and prominently displayed signs.

'Sorry, Miss Develin.'

'What are you sorry for, exactly?' she asks, her eyes narrowing. 'For calling me Ms Develin, or for downloading songs?'

'The first thing. We weren't downloading songs.'

'Because if you were ...'

And she tilts her head towards the Door.

It's the only threat she needs.

I've seen someone come out of the Door just once. It was during a presentation by some old bush poet. Don't ask me about bush poetry, I wasn't really listening. What I do remember is that as soon as I heard him say that he was going to recite some bush poetry for us, I switched off. If bush poetry is about the bush, then I'm not interested, since I've only ever been there once, and I hated it. And if bush poetry is intended for reciting in the bush, then why have someone recite it at our school, which is, by any estimation, in the middle of the city?

So he was reciting poetry that was possibly about the bush — but definitely not in the bush — and I was carefully sending a text to Briony, who was away sick that day. I had my phone tucked between my knees, hidden in the pleated folds of my skirt, and I'd just sent the text when Clare nudged me with her elbow.

I looked up. My heart was already lurching, because I fully expected to see a teacher glaring at me. But no. Clare was nodding towards the bottom of the library. Towards the Door, which had just clicked shut in that very efficient, steel door-frames, self-closing, brand-new library kind of way.

But of more interest was the shadowy movement behind the periodicals shelves. In the gaps between the cardboard magazine files with the little laminated signs I saw a passing shape, hunched over, lurching slightly. Its footsteps padded along behind the shelving, and a smell drifted through and around the magazines, rising to me like an invisible mist. I felt revulsion rising, and a shudder passed through one shoulder, across the nape of my neck, and down the other arm.

Then it coughed. It was a kind of gurgling rasp, and every girl in that room caught her breath. They all turned to see what Clare and I had already seen — the shape emerging from between the *Newsweek*s and the *National Geographic*s.

And it stood there, gawping at us with its red, sun-starved eyes.

The bush poet hesitated mid-line, tried again, then stopped a second time. He frowned at the figure that was regarding him evenly, its breath made up of very faint, slightly wet wheezes.

'Can I help you?' asked the poet, his voice low and

even, like he was facing a wild boar or a water buffalo or a deadly snake, out in his precious bush.

Then the figure spoke, in a surprisingly quiet voice.

'Don't mind me,' it said. 'I've just got to tidy up some of these PCs.' It turned slowly, and stared deep into the soul of every girl in that room. 'Someone's been downloading songs again.'

Vincent

Alistair Wood

MY NAME is Vincent
I prey on the innocent
As quiet as a mouse
I came upon a house
I opened the front door in the middle
of the night
Oh such a scare, they will get such
a fright!
As I walked up the stairs there
were lightning flashes
I thought I heard a footstep so I
made quick dashes
The saliva dripped from my mouth
cold and thin
And across my face crept a sinister grin
I saw a door behind which was a glow
Their end will come so fast
they won't even know.
I opened the door and everyone screamed
'Happy Halloween!' as their faces beamed.

POPE:
Operation Delivery
Ella Sexton
Illustration by Shaun Tan

'**HERE TAKE** it, quickly.'

He looped it over my neck and tucked it under my thick black jacket so only the worn leather band was visible.

'Have you got the directions?' I asked.

'Yeah, here,' he said, as he fished a crumpled piece of paper out of his pocket and pressed it into my outstretched hand. 'It's about a twenty minute walk from here. Hurry, he will be waiting. You have to get there before the Shadowmen come. You know what this means to the organisation: we're depending on you.'

I nodded.

'Go now, quickly! I think I can hear them coming. I'll try leading them off in the other direction. Be careful, stay safe.' He whispered and forced a reassuring smile, before he melted into the darkness and disappeared.

I turned and walked quickly in the opposite direction. The full moon loomed on the horizon, half-hidden by clouds. I strode over to the nearest street lamp, smoothing out the paper as I went. I peered down at the faint curly handwriting, straining my eyes to see under the dim glow of the light.

Of course it was all in code, as was almost everything that was written down in the POPE — Protection Of People Everywhere — organisation, if it was written down at all. Mostly messages were communicated via the use of messengers and information committed to memory. POPE members were well drilled when it came to security.

I sat on the gutter and took a few minutes to decode the directions. I read over it a few times to be sure I knew it by heart, before ripping it into tiny pieces and depositing them into five different bins. Standard POPE precaution. The icy wind ripped through me as it swept by, forcing trees to bend to its all too powerful force. I wrapped my arms around myself, rubbing my upper left arm where, under my thick black jacket, the Celtic cross branded me a POPE agent for life.

I wondered again if I'd made the right choice by

joining POPE. Not that it had been a choice at the time. I had found out about the organisation, which left me with only two options as they had quite simply explained. I could join or I could die.

I knew what they — no we — did was for the protection and safety of people everywhere. It was just that sometimes, or to be more accurate, often, when doing things for the greater good you have to make sacrifices. What was one life to a hundred?

I jumped as an owl hooted loudly snapping me back to reality. I turned the corner and glanced around, noticing my surroundings for the first time. A few ramshackle houses lined the road, overgrown with weeds and long grass. On the right side of the street behind a high barbed wire fence was a large rundown factory. Numerous windows were smashed and bright red and orange graffiti featured prominently on its bare grey walls. The roar of a car echoed in the distance breaking the eerie silence gripping the road. The lone street lamp flickered and died. I was completely immersed in darkness. I shivered, hesitating for the slightest moment before I continued onward, walking faster this time. I heard footsteps behind me and increased pace again. Beads of sweat gathered on my forehead as I tried to calm myself. The footsteps were too even, careful and quiet. It was the Shadowmen and they were after me, or rather, what I had hung around my neck.

I fingered the heavy, gold medallion beneath my jacket, wondering again what was so special about it. Why was it causing such a stir? The Shadowmen usually never came this close to open conflict. But being merely a pawn in the scheme of things nobody bothered to mention what exactly it was that I was risking my life for today.

Another pair of footsteps joined the ones behind me and then another and another and another. My heart pounded as I increased my pace yet again. I couldn't let them catch me. I scanned the street looking urgently for some means of escape. I spotted a gloomy alleyway and headed straight for it. As soon as I reached the entrance I broke straight into a run. I winced as my feet clattered along the cobblestones, sounding oddly strange and loud in the silence of the night. The Shadowmen's footsteps became faster as they pursued me, gaining on me as every second passed. I had to keep running. My breaths were coming in long, rasping gasps now as I continued to

force my feet to keep moving. I had a sharp, stabbing pain in my chest and my legs felt ready to collapse at any moment.

The alleyway finally came out at a small river and I ran along the wide pathway winding beside it. I felt totally isolated. I considered calling out for help, but I strongly doubted anyone would hear me. The Shadowmen had caught up with me now and some overtook me, encircling me, forcing me to stop. I looked around at the tall black-cloaked figures surrounding me, the expressions on their faces obliterating any last remnants of hope I might have had. As one last act out of desperation, I pulled the medallion over my head, balled it up in my fist and using my last reserves of strength, threw it into the river, where the current quickly pulled it downstream and around the bend as it slowly sank towards the bottom.

My legs trembled with exhaustion and buckled beneath me, no longer able to bear my weight. Dizziness filled my head and my vision wavered as I tried to fight off the darkness threatening to envelop me.

And I waited for them to come.

Twisted Fairytales
Rachel Holkner

Honey

A girl with curly blonde hair sat at the breakfast table.
She dipped her finger into a bowl of porridge. Too
hot. She was about to pour from the jug of milk onto
the second bowl when the front door opened. A furry
head peered around. 'You were right to leave the door
open, Mother,' it growled. 'Lunch has arrived.'

Signal

Grandmother put the last stitches in place and broke
off the thread with her teeth. She smoothed the cape
out before her, admiring her work, then parcelled it
up carefully, tied a ribbon and wrote 'Happy Birthday'.
That will attract them, she thought. Granddaughter
will be a walking red flag.

Crumbs

'We shall all four of us surely starve,' said the cruel wife as they made their way further into the woods.

'You are right,' said the woodcutter and he raised his axe.

He and his young son and daughter ate well through the winter.

Although they tired of the flavour after a while.

Seed

An old man sold him magic beans and the boy ate them. Overnight a tree grew through his body. A slim trunk grew from his mouth and roots exited his backside. He was clamped to the floor of his bedroom. The plant sought water through the foundations of the house making it unstable. Leaves brushed the ceiling, colouring the light and casting shadows.

'We'll wait,' his mother said, 'And see what the harvest is like.'

Crocodile Tears

Margaret Crohn

MAT AND Jason sauntered to the viewing platform of the wildlife park. In front of them the murky swamp gurgled quietly.

'I dare you,' said Jason.

Mat tapped on the glass that separated the visitors from the animals. A gnarled piece of wood floated on the surface just in front of him.

'Boring,' said Jason. 'Do it harder.'

Mat used his fist to bang louder on the glass and the piece of wood opened one yellow eye and stared at him.

Jason laughed. 'That's better. Wake him up, the lazy bludger.'

Mat cupped his hands and yelled. 'Oiy.'

The croc sleepily opened its other eye.

A wildlife ranger hurried up to the boys. 'Hey, can't you read. It says don't knock on the glass. These animals have very sensitive hearing. That really upsets them.'

Jason laughed. 'I'm not afraid,' he sneered. 'Crocs aren't dangerous. I've got this awesome computer game at home, Monster Crocs Wrestling and I always win. Easy.'

'These aren't computer animations,' said the ranger. 'These are mighty creatures, and they'd have you for breakfast,' he said as he hoisted up his khaki shorts. 'And they remember,' he said ominously.

He glared at Mat then spotted another group of visitors leaning over the fence and hurried off to deal with them.

Jason watched the ranger walk away. He picked up a long stick and leaned over the glass panel. He waved the stick close to the crocodile's toothy snout and chanted, 'Come and get your breakfast, come and get it.' He chuckled, and nudged Mat in the ribs, 'That's more like it.'

The croc raised its head out of the slimy water and showed a row of sharp teeth poking out from its closed jaws. It blinked once, twice, then silently dropped back into the water and slid away. Only a ripple showed where it had been.

'Huh,' said Jason. 'It couldn't take the pressure. Not as gutsy as the Monster Crocs. We should've stayed at home and killed them all on the computer game.'

'Let's go home,' Mat murmured. 'We've seen all the animals today.'

'Seen 'em?' said Jason. 'Shown 'em who's boss, more like it. Boo hoo, poor little croccys.' He pretended to wipe away some tears.

Behind the glass, several crocs slid off the bank into the lagoon and their silent ripples followed the first croc across the water.

Jason woke with a start. He panicked for a moment, sure he was being held underwater in a croc's death roll. But then he realised he was only tangled in his own damp sheets, soaked in sweat from his fright.

He unrolled the sheets and sat up on the edge of his bed. He listened carefully. There was a strange hissing coming from the corner of the room. Jason switched on the bedside light and crept over to his desk. The hissing seemed to be coming from the computer. He checked the modem, but the power was off.

Suddenly the screen lit up and the Monster Crocs Wrestling homepage appeared. Jason shivered and his palms began to sweat. He hadn't touched the keyboard. On the screen, the giant crocodile rolled and snapped as the game loaded. Its jaws clashed as it grabbed a fish and swallowed it whole. Its eyes flashed, as the animation became a close-up of its head. Larger and larger, closer and closer the scaly croc's head, eyes, jaws and teeth loomed as the graphics zoomed in.

Jason screamed.

The croc was smashing out of the screen. It was crashing across the desk, its ferocious head followed by a thick neck and massive body. Its webbed feet were scrabbling on the chair and its chunky tail was swinging wildly from side to side as it finally emerged completely from the computer monitor and lumbered into Jason's bedroom.

Its jaws were wide open and its teeth shone with saliva, as its yellow eyes fixed unblinkingly on the boy. Jason backed away from the fearsome creature, into the far corner of the room, while the crocodile lashed its tail, scattering books and shoes. It lifted the rug and knocked over the bedside lamp.

The light globe shattered and the room fell dark. Only the glow of the computer screen showed Jason where the croc was, as it trod purposefully towards him. And then that light flickered as another croc slid out of the screen, and then another and then a third.

And as they flicked their heads, small tears dripped onto the floor.

Apparition

Donna Smith

NO ONE THERE I see,

A space that appears empty

A chill surrounds me...

Garlic Cake

Carolyn Nguyen

MY SISTER'S dating a vampire.

At first, I didn't realise. I just thought he was a weirdo who wore mascara and painted his fingernails black and quoted stuff from olden day poets like John Keats and Lord Byron. But then I found out about his garlic problem. When he eats garlic, he goes red and blistery and looks exactly like sheep's brain that's been left out for too long in the sun.

I began to notice other things too. How he always plasters himself with sunscreen before going outside. And he always kisses my sister on the neck instead of on the lips like real boyfriends do.

My sister doesn't care. The mascara and black fingernails and Keats and Byron make her like him even more. He's probably fixed some vampire voodoo on her. Whenever she talks to him on the phone, she puts on an eerie high-pitched voice that makes her sound like a dolphin.

I tried to prove that he was a vampire.

One time I stole his Coke bottle and got the crazy guy who preaches in the Coles car park to bless it. Then I snuck the bottle back into the boyfriend's schoolbag. But when he wolfed the syrupy stuff down, he didn't smoke up or catch fire or anything, and I wondered how he had manage to survive the holy Coke. I suppose he must have just pretended to drink it. After all, vampires only drink blood, right?

So then I thought of a better plan. My sister was baking him a cake for Valentine's Day. She was putting a lot of effort into it, so he was going to have to finish the whole lot. While she was busy lining the cake tin, I tipped a jar of minced garlic into the mixing bowl.

Having set the vampire trap, I sat and waited. My sister hummed along to MTV, slathering icing over her coffee-and-pumpkin flavoured disasterpiece. She even thanked me for helping her mix the milk and eggs and flour together. After she finished decorating the cake, she rushed upstairs and smeared on some red lipstick. Her mouth looked like it was rimmed with blood.

The vampire boyfriend turned up with a bunch of flowers he stole from the cemetery. Or so I'm guessing. Mum and Dad were out for dinner, so it was just us three watching Home and Away. He tried to neck my sister when he thought I wasn't watching.

'I made something for you,' my sister told him, pushing him away.

She went into the kitchen and came back with a cake frosted in black icing. On the icing, in white wobbly letters, were the words 'Happy Valentine's Day'. She cut one big slice for him and one small slice for herself and told me to get lost.

I pretended to go to my room but ducked behind the curtains instead.

The vampire necked her again. My sister carved a chunk out of 'Happy' and offered it to him. He opened his mouth to reveal pointy canines. His pale lips closed over the fork and cake.

And he chewed.

There was a pause. Then the cake slapped onto the floor as the vampire ran over to the kitchen sink.

Five minutes later my sister found me. Her nails dug into my arm. She dragged me up the stairs.

'You put garlic in the cake,' she yelled. 'You know Seb's allergic to garlic.'

'That's because he's a vampire,' I yelled back.

Then I listed the reasons why he was a vampire.

1.   You could see the web of veins underneath his skin.

2.   There was always dirt under his nails as if he'd just clawed his way out of a grave.

3.   He still listened to audio cassettes.

My sister glared at me.

'In that case, I'm also a vampire. Get lost, you freak.'

I started eating garlic every day after that. I eat a tablespoon with breakfast, lunch and dinner, even though it makes my tummy queasy and my farts nuclear. It's the only protection I have against my vampire sister and her vampire boyfriend.

Sometimes I see them walking through the cemetery near our house. Apart from their handholding, they look like twins with their black clothes and their black hair and their black nails. They talk about stuff that my sister and I used to talk about

— before she went bad.

And when they whisper, leaning in close towards each other, I wish I were a vampire too.

Tilt
Stewart Bishop

AS THE sun slowly receded behind the mountains, and the last whispers of light started to fade into the shadows, a boy opened a gate, and walked down a garden path towards the black silhouette of an old house.

The door was creaky. That was the first thing he noticed as he stepped inside. The floor was creaky, too. Every step he took he heard again in the groaning of the wood.

The entire house gave him the creeps.

He wanted to turn back, to run away, though he knew that he couldn't, he couldn't go back now.

The first thing he saw was blood splattered across the rug and the walls and the floors. He thought he heard a scream. He wished it was his own.

It wasn't.

The boy scanned the room. The one thing that seemed to be alive was the fire. It crackled, and lashed out at him. He stumbled. Then he fell. Then everything went black. The last thing the boy saw was the crackling fire and it seemed to consume him.

He opened his eyes with a start and noticed a photo frame on a small table. In the photo, an old man posed in front of the very house the boy was in. It looked newer than now, and the sky behind the house was almost black. The old man looked as if he were trying to tell the boy something. The man's eyes were wide and bloodshot, and although he was still, he looked as if he, too, wanted to run away.

The windows of the house behind him were brightly lit.

The boy glanced back to the fire, and wanted to yell out, but he found he couldn't. He couldn't do anything. And once again the fire seemed to consume him.

Through the window he could see a storm. He took a moment to stare out.

Outside.

Then the window got smaller and smaller. Outside, the storm strengthened, but he didn't care. He didn't want to be anywhere but outside the house.

Suddenly the last few hours of his life flashed before his eyes. But had they been hours? Or days? Years, even?

The door, creaking as he opened it.

The blood, splattered across the rug and the walls and the floor.

The terrifying scream that he had wished was his.

The fireplace, seemingly the only alive thing in the house.

The man in the photo, the look on his face.

Outside.

The fire.

The fire consumed him again.

The old man woke up and stared at the ceiling.

He cautiously stood up and looked around.

He took the photo frame off the small table in the corner of the room. And looked at the young man in the picture, his eyes frozen with fear, the windows of the house behind him brightly lit.

Tumbleweeds
Aleesah Darlison

THE THREE friends had been arguing the whole way home. Squiggly had led them on a short cut through the forest, even though everyone knew the forest was enchanted.

'I think we should have gone the other way,' said Rhyll for the fourth time.

'That takes ages,' argued Squiggly.

As they rounded a bend they stopped in surprise. Perched on top of a huge bolder beside the forest trail sat a huge figure smoking a pipe. It was a toad.

'Is that what I think it is?' said Squiggly.

Tane squinted. 'Can't be.'

'Let's turn back,' Rhyll whispered.

'Too late. That thing has seen us. And, it's waving.'

The three friends approached the boulder warily.

'Will, will, what have we here? Little chl'dun.'

Tane snorted. 'Not so much of the little, thanks.'

'Ah, no, a' course not. I am mostly sorry. Let me introduce myself. My name is Tumbleweed Tarnicious Toad and I'm mostly pleased to make yer 'quaintance. What be yor names, then?'

'This is Tane and Rhyll,' said Squiggly, 'and I'm Squiggly. That's Trip, my dog.'

'Is that so? And a mostly delightful dog he is, too.' Tumbleweed's tongue flicked left and right. 'Doesn't lend to biting does 'e Squiggles?'

'It's Squiggly, and no, he doesn't bite.'

Tumbleweed slid down from the boulder and stood up, his rubbery legs spread wide to balance his huge bulk. 'That's good, that is.' He watched the friends with dark, swampy eyes.

The giant toad placed his rubbery hand on Squiggly's shoulder. His fingers were round and soggy like rotting onions and smelled like them, too. Squiggly felt their clammy wetness seep through his shirt and he tried not to shudder.

'Why don't you child'un come with me?' Tumbleweed's voice was all syrup.

'We're just passing through,' said Squiggly, trying to tear his eyes away from the pumpkin-sized warts on the toad's chin. 'We should be on our way.'

'Will, no one passes through here without saying hello to my dear missus. She'll be dining to meet you… I mean, you'll die when she eats… I mean, she'll be dying to meet you. Besides, before you know it, it'll be dark and there are hordes of gigantic vampire bats in these parts.'

'Bigger than you?' Tane asked.

Tumbleweed rested his other hand on Tane's shoulder and squeezed. Hard.

Tane whimpered.

'Almost, child, almost.'

'Mrs Toad!' Tumbleweed called into the mouth of an overgrown burrow. 'Visitors!'

Out of the hole lumbered another enormous toad wearing a muddy dress and a strand of river rocks around her neck.

'Why, Tumbleweed, what have we here?' Mrs Toad puffed her chin out. Her necklace strained under the pressure.

'I've brought you some child'un.'

Mrs Toad clapped her hands together. A blob of toad-slick shot through the air and landed in Tane's hair. Tane tried to wipe it away, but only succeeded in making his hands sticky.

'Why, Tumbleweed, you are a mostly thoughtful husband.' Mrs Toad smacked a slobbering kiss on Tumbleweed's lips then turned to the friends. 'My last batch of taddies got washed away in the summer rains. Been on our own ever since, we have.' Mrs Toad dabbed her eyes with her tongue, as if it were a handkerchief.

'But Tumbleweed is such a thoughtful dear, he knew I was missing them. How kind of him to bring me some child'un to play with.'

Drool slipped off Mrs Toad's giant lips and down her dress.

Squiggly glanced at Tane and Rhyll and saw his own terror reflected in their eyes. Trip whined and stayed outside.

'Come inside, child'un.' Tumbleweed waved his pipe at them. 'Mrs Toad will rustle you up as snacks... I mean, rustle you up some snacks to eat.'

Mrs Toad tittered. 'Why, yes, of course. I always keep the larder well stocked. Just finished pickling a batch of dung beetles, I did. Never know when one might get visitors, might one, Tumbleweed?'

'That's mostly right, my dear. Now, come child'un, into the hole.'

Rhyll stared into the black tunnel. 'Down there?'

'Don't let the dark put you off.' Tumbleweed nudged her forward. 'It really is comfortable.'

Rhyll gulped. 'I'm not good in tight spaces.'

'Don't worry yer pretty head about it.' Mrs Toad tugged her arm.

Rhyll turned to Squiggly. 'I knew we should have taken the other path!' she hissed.

'It's not too late,' Squiggly said.

'For what?' Rhyll wrestled her arm free from Mrs Toad's grasp.

'To run!'

It was all they needed. Squiggly, Tane and Rhyll tore through the forest with Trip close behind.

'Stop them!' Mrs Toad screamed.

'Come back here, yer villains!' Tumbleweed crashed through the trees. 'Wait till I catch yers!'

The giant toad lumbered after them, but he was so big and cumbersome that the friends soon lost him. In their haste to escape, however, they didn't see the gigantic cobweb strung across the path. The instant they stumbled into it, they were stuck fast.

'I think we should have gone the other way,' said Rhyll for the fifth time that day.

The Last Spam

Kerry Munnery

I AM SITTING at my computer. The clock at the
bottom of the screen says 4.21AM.

Then 4.22AM, 4.23AM.

My eyelids droop. My bed is right there in the
corner, with the doona thrown back and the soft
pillow beckoning. The desire to crawl in and draw the
covers over my head is overwhelming.

But I can not.

I sit here with my fingertips resting on the keys
and the glare of the screen burning my eyes.

My family sleeps quietly in the rooms around me.

I was sound asleep myself when a beam of light shot
out from my computer. I always turn everything off —

speakers, screen, everything — otherwise I cop it from my step-mum.

'Turn it off at the powerpoint. Save the planet, blah, blah, blah.'

The beam of greenish-white light was just bright enough to keep me awake. I heaved myself out of bed, tripping over the sheet.

I squinted at the computer, which sat in one corner of my room. A single ray of light beamed from the middle of the screen. Then it changed. The single beam kind of melted and spread. It formed letters. First there was an H. Then an I.

'Hi?' I thought.

The letters disappeared and then some more appeared. 'Cool, yeah?'

I grinned. I figured it was Jack, my computer nerd friend. He spent every spare minute fiddling with electronic things. He'd obviously found a way to turn on my computer and send a message via remote control.

'Check your email!' the letters commanded.

I turned on the computer. Sure enough, there was an email.

I grabbed the mouse.

I clicked on the message.

Stupid, I know, but it was the middle of the night and I was half-asleep.

As I clicked on the message, I jumped. A strange feeling shot up my arm, like when I accidentally touch the electric fence at my uncle's farm, but milder.

Maybe something was wrong with my computer?

'I HAVE YOU NOW!' the words formed in huge light-letters on the screen.

Very amusing, Jack. Not, I thought.

I thought I'd talk to him in the morning. I half-stood.

'NO!' The letters were almost as big as the screen and blindingly white.

'SIT!'

I felt uneasy, but found myself sitting down. I tried to draw my hands away from the keyboard, but they wouldn't move.

This was no special trick from Jack.

These messages were not from any friend of mine.

'TYPE,' the screen commanded.

'Type what?' I typed. I seemed to have lost the ability to talk.

'ANYTHING,' commanded the screen.

'NO,' I typed back.

Another bolt of pain travelled up my arm. I would have cried out if I could.

I typed.

'SEND IT TO YOUR FRIENDS,' commanded the screen.

I tried to resist. I really did.

But I think you will understand, if you are reading this now, how useless it is to try and resist.

By now you will have written your own message. Sent it to your own friends.

By now I expect it is on its way around the world.

We are in its control. Whatever it is. Wherever it is from.

I am sitting in the dark with no control over my hands. My family sleeps in the rooms all around me.

My neighbours sleep in their houses in the quiet suburb where I live.

Except, perhaps here and there, where a computer screen flickers into life on its own accord.

And as I sit and wait, words are forming on my screen.

I have to go.

They are waiting.

The Biology Lesson

June Gleeson

'**WELCOME,**' **BARKED** a hoarse dark voice. 'I sensed something coming.' He peered short-sightedly at me with his two central eyes. 'A young human! Splendid!'

A metre-high spider squatted behind me against the closed door. Instinctively I moved forward to avoid the purplish black creature.

Stupid, stupid move Jake Henderson. Now you're trapped. And nobody knows where you are.

I'd skipped last period — biology — to meet someone after school, but I'd obviously got the address wrong. Toxic fangs close to my spine, the spider edged me down a passageway into a brilliantly-lit room stretching across the whole house.

I gaped. Glass containers holding twisted carcasses

lined the walls. I smelled formaldehyde. Weirdly
shaped tissues were pinned to boards. A gurney
stood in the centre, straps loose. A sterilizer steamed
nearby. A mass of rubble had been gathered into a
pile near the window. Further back, a dense white
tubular web funneled down into a crevice.

'You've noticed my specimens?' The hoarse voice
was arch. 'Twenty years' experimentation — part
of the Arachnid Research and Breeding Program. I
myself am a product of that program.' He preened.

'Growth hormones and gene therapy increased my
poisons, size and intelligence, and gave me a voice;
and now I can live anywhere. Dr Thoracicus, Sydney
funnel web, version 125, male. And specialist in egg
implantation and gene therapy. I learned my skills
from the wasps that used us as hosts and food supply
for their eggs.' He bowed.

'You will be very significant to the Arachnid
Program. I want to implant human genes into our
spiderlings. A young, fit body like yours will provide
excellent food, and donor genes for spiderlings.
You'll be conscious and know what's happening;
unfortunately it will be painful. I regret the pain,'
he barked insincerely. 'But our species deserves

more honour. I will ensure I receive respect — and obedience.' His eyes glowed.

His aggression overwhelmed me. Eggs hatching inside me, thousands of funnel webs biting, feeding on me? I couldn't think. Excruciating pain as atraxotoxins attacked my nervous system, sweating and convulsing, respiratory failure, paralysis, all imminent. And gene extraction? My limbs trembled, my brain whirled. I felt powerless, terrified. I wanted to shout for help but that would be useless.

Stupidly, I tried spelling Thoracicus. That woke me up. I wouldn't let him do as he pleased. But what could I do? I was backed against a rotting window frame, with broken trash and barbed wire from the encircling factories outside below. Jump, and he could collect the bits.

The evil creature reared ready to strike. If he pinned me with his fangs he'd not let go. Goodbye Jake.

I could distract him. But how? Thoracicus's vision was poor. He felt my vibrations through his foot and skin sensors. Could I make vibrations elsewhere?

I sat heavily on the windowsill, putting all my weight on the edge. It split with a loud crack. I grabbed and threw the broken plank to the far side of the gurney. It fell heavily. Surprised, the spider half-turned toward the sound. I slipped behind him along the wall toward the door.

But I was not to escape his powerful fangs so easily. Sensing movement, he wheeled back. He appeared not to see me flat against the wall, the gurney between us. I heaved the gurney broadside over him, hoping the clatter and confusion would stop him. I grabbed a metal stake from the pile of rubble, I'd have to kill him. I couldn't raise an alert. Nobody would believe me.

'Another story, Jake?'

Where was the monster vulnerable? His head or cephalorax housed his brain, poison glands and sucking stomach. His abdomen held his heart and other organs. If I made a deep slit, Thoracicus would bleed to death. Start at the head to incapacitate the poisonous fangs, and jab downwards through the abdomen. I'd have to be quick to avoid the fangs' pickaxe thrust. There'd only be one chance.

He paused, feeling for my vibrations. I sneezed!

The spider swiveled toward me, two central eyes searching. Keep still Jake. He crept closer. He must have sensed my breath. Suddenly he reared, towering above me, fangs plunging down. I lunged forward and drove home the stake like a javelin, dropped immediately to pull it through the abdomen, then slashed and skittered sideways to avoid the fangs' venomous descent. A huge gash opened through his lower head and underbelly. Thoracicus staggered, fangs closing on the floor immediately behind me. I crawled towards the door then watched as Thoracicus's legs buckled and he sank like a deflated balloon.

When I finally reached home, Mum stopped me as I slipped into my bedroom.

'Where've you been Jake?' she asked.

'Just studying biology, Mum.'

The Moth-er

Lili Wilkinson

I'M A MOTH-ER.

Not a mother, you see. No. A moth-er. One who studies moths. A lepidopterist, if you will.

A lot of people are scared of moths, and rightly so, although it's often for the wrong reasons. Have you ever wondered why? I mean, they're just the same as butterflies, right?

Wrong.

Butterflies are like the glitzy trailer trash of the lepidoptera family. All fancy and shiny and brightly coloured.

Not moths. Moths are strange and beautiful and subtle. And dangerous.

Have you ever seen a moth dance around a light? Some people say it's because they do something called celestial navigation, where they use the position of the moon to fly in a straight line. But they get all confused when they come across a light globe or a candle, which is much smaller and closer than the moon, and spiral around it, all flapping and buzzing.

Except that isn't really why they're attracted to the light.

I became a moth-er when I was eight or nine years old. My mother was terrified of moths, and would squash them with her shoe or a rolled-up newspaper. It was the dust, she said. The moth-dust on their wings. If you got it in your eyes you'd go blind.

I thought she was being silly. What harm could a tiny sprinkling of moth-dust do? Little did I know.

Maybe it was because moths were so unwelcome in our house. Maybe it was something else. I don't know why, but I became fascinated with them. I'd sit in the back garden at twilight with a candle, still as still, watching the moths spiral and dive towards the flame.

Just as they were drawn to the light, I was drawn

to them. Their soft, furry bodies and delicate subtle
wings. I learned to recognise them by the shape
of their bodies, and the markings on their wings. I
learned to call them by name.

The Oleander hawkmoth, green and black like
an alien. The Scalloped Oak moth with its sad black
bead eyes and striped mask. The Elephant hawkmoth,
patterned with khaki and magenta fur. And the
Spirama retorta, its wings a hypnotic dazzle of zigzags
and spirals in browns and blacks and blues.

I knew them all, and soon enough, they knew me.

It began out there, in the back garden with the
candle.

One night, my candle blew out. I was out of
matches, and would have gone inside to bed, except
the night was mild and the sky was clear. So I sat for
a moment.

And the moths came.

They weren't coming for the candle, this time.
They were coming for me. They fluttered and spiraled
out of the sky down to me, landing on my arms, my
cheeks, my eyelids. Their soft bodies brushed against
my skin, their wings quivered, and I was showered in
the finest, most delicate layer of moth-dust.

My mother was wrong. Moth dust doesn't make you blind.

Quite the opposite, in fact.

For the first time, I could really see. I could see every glimmer of light, all over the world. And the stars. Stars, stretching off into oblivion.

And I understood. All my life, this is what I'd been waiting for. This one thing.

Then, on that night, I never thought it would bring me so far. Bring me here.

Do you think you could turn that siren off? It's very loud. Could you tell me how? Which button? There are so many. This one? Ah. That's better.

The thing I said before? About celestial navigation? It's a bit more complicated than that. And it's got nothing to do with the moon. It's all about the stars. And the moths aren't trying to navigate with the stars. They're trying to navigate to the stars.

They want to go home.

I'm telling you this so you'll understand. So you won't be frightened by what comes next. They always get frightened. It makes things so much worse. All the running around and screaming. If you didn't all jump in your cars as soon as things start getting interesting, then you wouldn't keep crashing into each other in the dark.

Listen. They're coming now. Can you hear them? No, of course you can't. Not yet. But you will.

Did you know that moths have no stomach? Most of them live for just a single day. Just a single day. Can you imagine? If you had just one day to live, what would you do?

They can't get home, you see. And it's our fault. It's hard to navigate to the stars when the planet is peppered with fake stars — light globes, candles, cities, fires, cars. It becomes like turning on a billion different radios, playing a billion different songs, and trying to pick out a single melody. Confusing.

That's why they chose me. And others like me. The moth-ers. We're everywhere, tonight. In places like this one, all over the country. We're going to help them get home.

You're going to help, too.

Now if you'll just sit still for a moment, still as still, while I turn out the lights.

Musical Chairs

By Maude Farrugia

About the Creators

LAURA BAHDUS-WILSON
Laura had a brilliant childhood and enjoys reliving it through
writing stories for children — particularly those involving tea
parties, stinky skunks, terrible tantrums and dogs who sneak
inside at night and scare the daylights out of little boys. In real
life she works as a Marketing Manager in the corporate world,
but sneaks off during lunch breaks to local cafes to scribble
down story ideas or sink into a good book.

KATHERINE BATTERSBY
Katherine is a children's author and illustrator whose first
picture book *Squish Rabbit* will be published by Viking
(Penguin US). She has had many short stories published in
magazines and recently won an Australian Society of Authors'
Mentorship to develop a junior fantasy novel. She loves
rabbits, running and anime and thinks exclamation marks are
evil.

TEGAN BELL
Tegan Bell has been in love with art and drawing since she
could hold a pencil. Now, at age 19, she draws every day.
Her preferred media includes coloured pencil, gouache and

watercolour and her most loved subject matter is people. Tegan is studying Fine Art at Monash University. She hopes to become a VCE art teacher and to continue illustrating books for children.

STEWART BISHOP
Stewart Bishop is in Year 8. He wrote this story when he was in Year 7, aged 11. He loves to read, come up with story ideas and write. His aim is to become a full-time writer.

ZOE BOYD
Zoe has always had an underlying wariness of clowns and an unbearable terror of butterflies and moths. She has been to the circus few times, but all visits have resulted in nightmares. She is in Year 11 and almost constantly writes or draws in her spare time. Zoe also spends an inordinate amount of time talking to her cat, who does not answer back in any understandable way. This is probably because she thinks Zoe would not understand her if she were to speak.

ANANDA BRAXTON-SMITH
Ananda Braxton-Smith is scared of most things. The dark. Toads and stick-insects. Sports Days. At school she was scared of other people, especially those who were good at sports or teasing, so she really enjoyed writing this spiteful little story. She hopes those people all read it now as grown-ups, and feel bad. Not bad enough to track her down and subject her to the terrible adult wedgie, though.

JANEEN BRIAN

Janeen Brian is an award-winning author of over 70 children's books. Her well-known titles include *Where does Thursday go?*, *Hoosh! Camels in Australia* and *Pilawuk — When I was Young*. She loves writing picture books, poetry and short fiction best of all. She also has over 100 stories and poems published in children's magazines. Janeen is an Ambassador for the SA Premier's Reading Challenge and reading is a passion. She also likes creating mosaics from recycled materials as well as gardening, swimming, fitness classes, watching films and plays and spending time with family and friends. Her little grey-and-white kitten is called Shonti.

STEPHANIE CAMPISI

Stephanie is a writer of the weird and sometimes wonderful. Her short stories have been published in magazines and anthologies worldwide, including in the US, the Czech Republic, Argentina and Singapore.

MEREDITH COSTAIN

Meredith lives in inner-city Melbourne with a menagerie of pets: five chooks, assorted goldfish, a cat and two cat-chasing dogs — a kelpie and a heeler. Her books include the series *A Year in Girl Hell*, *Dog Squad* and *Doodledum Dancing*. Although there are bats in her belfry, there are definitely no monsters under her bed (she's checked, often).

MARGARET CROHN

Margaret has been writing stories, articles and book reviews for children and young people since late last century. She loves researching articles and often gets sidetracked discovering fascinating but useless facts. Thank goodness for deadlines, or she would never finish writing anything. Many of her stories come from things she has heard or seen children do in the many years she has been a mother and a teacher. She wrote *Crocodile Tears* after she took her children, who love computer games, to the zoo, and wondered what would happen if she combined both activities.

ALEESAH DARLISON

Aleesah writes stories for children and young adults and reviews books for the *Herald Sun*. Her first picture book, *The Diary of Persephone Pinchgut*, is due for release this year. When she isn't writing, she's usually taking her three children on marvellous adventures.

TERRY DENTON

Terry is one of Australia's busiest literary creative forces. He lives by the beach with his wife and three kids, two dogs, a few chooks and a huge burial mound of previous pets—but no little bottoms!

MAUDE FARRUGIA

Maude grew up with 12 Derwent pencils in a little house by the sea. She now lives in Melbourne with a 36 set. One day she hopes to circumnavigate the world by freighter ship and sing in Eurovision (not at the same time).

SUSANNE GERVAY

Susanne Gervay's much-loved books include her Jack books — *I Am Jack*, *Super Jack* and *Always Jack*. *I Am Jack*, on school bullying, has been adapted into a play by the award-winning Monkey Baa Theatre. Her young adult books include the internationally recognised *Butterflies*, *The Cave* and *That's Why I Wrote This Song* melding songs into story.

HEATHER GALLAGHER

Heather has spent more than ten years working as a journalist for publications including *the Age*, *the Melbourne Times* and the *Northcote Leader*. She now writes for children full time. *The Hunt* is sadly inspired by the deaths of her own chickens.

JUNE GLEESON

June Gleeson is older than she would like to be, and is very scared of spiders, especially those that hide in dark corners and under pots. She likes to write stories and reads as many books as she can.

ANDY GRIFFITHS

Andy Griffiths is one of Australia's funniest writers for children. His books have sold over 4 million copies worldwide, have featured on the *New York Times* bestseller lists, and have won over 40 Australian children's choice awards.

SHERYL GWYTHER

Sheryl is a Queensland writer. She loves reading and writing adventure books, school plays and magazine articles. This is her first scary story and it even scared her while she was writing it. She has twice been the recipient of an Australian Society of Authors' Mentorship. Her latest releases are *Princess Clown* and *Charlie and the Red Hot Chilli Pepper*.

BEN HARMER

This story was written by Ben when he was in Year 7. He is now in Year 8 and loves writing stories and poetry. He loves books about quests and mystery and adventure and one day dreams of becoming a famous author writing books for children and teenagers.

HOLLY HARPER

Holly Harper is the world's foremost authority on procrastination. Her first-hand knowledge of this topic includes, but is not limited to: window-staring, monster-scribbling, cat-chasing, treasure-hunting and I'm-going-to-rearrange-the-furniture-instead-of-writing. When she's not procrastinating, she works in a bookshop as the children's specialist. This means she gets to spend her days around wonderful books like *Short and Scary*. Holly is working on an eight book series which is due to be published mid-2011.

AMY HAWLEY

In a prior life Amy Hawley painstakingly trained a flock of ducks to quack the chorus of Beethoven's *Ode to Joy*. In this one she likes to write stories. Who can say which life was time better spent? Certainly this one hasn't involved being covered in as many feathers or duck droppings.

REBECCA HAYMAN

Rebecca Hayman grew up on a farm in country Victoria with dogs, cats, horses, muddy dams and pretty much everything that makes for an adventure-filled childhood. She loves camping, canoeing and creating stories.

RACHEL HOLKNER

Rachel lives in Melbourne with her husband and daughter. She likes to write but doesn't know why her stories always come out scary. In her spare time she enjoys reading and making things. This year she is studying to be a librarian.

GUY HOLT

Guy was born in England and grew up on the North Cornish coast, where he still returns whenever he can. Now in Melbourne, whenever he is not working on his iMac he is playing games on his PS3, or listening to music on his iPhone. When not working he loves to escape the city, but the iPhone is always near at hand

JACKIE HOSKING

Jackie has been writing for children for five years. She writes short stories and poetry and especially likes to rhyme. Her work has been published both in Australia and overseas. Jackie enjoys editing other people's poems and edits and compiles the children's writing and illustrating industry newsletter, *Pass It On*.

GEORGE IVANOFF

George Ivanoff is a Melbourne-based author and stay-at-home dad. He likes reading and writing science fiction, fantasy and horror. He spends way too much time on the Internet, especially on Facebook and Twitter. His latest book is a teen sci-fi novel, *Gamers' Quest*.

BARRY JONSBERG

Barry Jonsberg is an award-winning author for young adults and children whose books have been translated into many languages. He lives in Darwin in the Northern Territory and is working on his first book for an adult audience.

MELISSA KEIL

Melissa has, at various times, been a tour guide, film student, drama teacher, Sangria-maker, phone answerer, and book editor. She hopes one day to write a long book, but needs to stop watching bad TV first. She is short, but not at all scary.

BERNADETTE KELLY

Bernadette Kelly is the author of the *Pony Patch* and the *Riding High* series. She wrote *Ute Man* after visiting a remote town in Tasmania. As far as she knows, Ute Man never existed, either in Tasmania or anywhere else. Bernadette lives in Victoria with her two children, six horses, a mouse-hunting dog and the laziest cat in the world.

JOSHUA KOPP

Joshua was born in 1997 and wrote this story in Year 7, aged 12. He is a second Dan black belt in Tae Kwon Do and enjoys fantasy novels, medieval weapons, Nerf Guns and games.

TALI LAVI

Tali has always been a dreamer. When she was at school, this wasn't always appreciated by her teachers but luckily now that she writes, it is considered an essential job requirement. Tali writes for people of all ages and is an avid collector of words and stories. She lives in Melbourne with her husband, two daughters and an ever-growing collection of books.

SUE LAWSON

Sue Lawson doesn't do scary at all well. Spontaneous combustion, clowns, werewolves and other things that go bump in the night terrify her. Rumour has it she was scared of escalators as a child. Just a little bit. And in her defence, she saw a child on TV caught in one. Sue refuses to watch horror movies. Sue's books include the *Diva* series, the award-winning *Allie McGregor's True Colours* and *Finding Darcy*. Her latest young adult book is *After*.

SHIRLEY MARR

Shirley Marr is a soon to be published novelist and loves being spooked and spooking others. She first freaked everyone out when as a baby she said she could see Grandpa's 'ghost'. She thinks cemeteries are peaceful and beautiful.

LORRAINE MARWOOD

Lorraine is a poet and children's author. She loves writing and believes in the power of poetry to express emotions and startling ideas. She likes to give voice to rural life and her latest book, *Star Jumps*, explores life on a dairy farm during drought.

MARC MCBRIDE

Marc McBride is the illustrator of the international best-selling children's book series *Deltora Quest*. He has also illustrated about 150 book covers and ten picture books. He has designed Dracula's castles in fun parks and is now an author with his 2007 picture book *World of Monsters*, which won the Science Fiction Aurealis award for best short fiction. His latest releases are the *Monster Book of Drawing* series.

HEATH MCKENZIE

Heath McKenzie is an illustrator of things both real and imaginary (handy, as his work in this book required a grasp of both). He has, to the best of his knowledge, never had an imaginary friend — he has some real ones though but if you ask them, they'll probably say he just imagined them...!

CHRIS MILES

Chris Miles writes books and things and builds websites. He is the author of *Who's on the Money?*, *Stuck on History* and *Explorers: Filling in the Map of Australia*. He has also had short fiction for adults published in print and online journals, and has worked as a magazine editor and feature writer.

JAMES MOLONEY

James loves writing books for kids and teenagers. He has written 32 of them so far including *The Book of Lies*, *The Gracey Trilogy*, and *A Bridge to Wiseman's Cove*, which won the Australian Children's Book Council Book of the Year Award in 1997.

KERRY MUNNERY

Kerry lives in Melbourne and writes stories for children and for adults. She has two children in Primary School and four very tall grown up step-children, and her household includes a dog, a cat, two guinea pigs, a rabbit and two mice who all get along famously. (Except the cats and mice who have to have separate rooms.) The idea for this story came about when someone said that computers had a 'hold' on children these days and she wondered what that might mean.

KELSEY MURPHY

Kelsey is 13 years old and currently in Year 8. Kelsey has always loved reading and writing stories and her favourite style is comical fiction. When she grows up she plans to study Creative Arts at university.

CAROLYN NGUYEN

Carolyn has completed a postgraduate diploma in Professional Writing at Deakin University. If asked to choose between *Buffy the Vampire Slayer* and *Twilight*, she'd pick Buffy every time.

SALLY ODGERS

Sally Odgers is a Tasmanian writer. She has a husband, two children, one grandson and a lot of dogs and books. She loves writing experimental verse such as *Don't Look*, which is a reversed acrostic.

MICHAEL PANCKRIDGE

Michael has only been writing since 2001 but already has 30 books to his credit. Recent novels include *The Cursed* and *The Vanishings*.

JARED PARKINSON

Jared Parkinson drew his headless monster last year in Year 7. He enjoys drawing and reading. He also likes manga such as *Naruto* and *Dragonball Z*. He likes to read fantasy books such as Terry Pratchett's *The Wee Free Men*.

SALLY RIPPIN

Sally was born in Darwin, Australia, but grew up mainly in South-East Asia. As an adult she studied traditional Chinese painting in China before moving to France with her family for three years. She now lives in Melbourne where she writes and illustrates for children of all ages. Sally has had over 30 children's books published, including two novels for Young Adults.

JAMES ROY

James Roy writes mostly for young people. He spends a lot of time writing and even more time travelling around talking about books, writing and what drives him as a writer. His short story collection *Town* won the Ethel Turner Prize in 2008, and his latest book is *Anonymity Jones*.

A. SEIB

Anke has been writing since she could hold a pen and hopes never to stop. She has never seen a ghost but wonders if people who have left our world can see us. That's what gave her the idea for *Regret*.

ELLA SEXTON

Ella wrote this story as a student in Year 8. She enjoys writing and is very excited to have Shaun Tan's illustration included with her story. She is currently in Year 9.

MATTHEW SHIRES

Matthew is an illustrator and author who is looking forward to a long career in children's books. He loves to draw monsters and characters of many themes. Watercolour, pastel and ink are some of his favourite mediums to use. Illustrating is something he has to do every day and he is currently working on a few other projects as variety is the spice of life.

CLARA BATTON SMITH

Clara Batton Smith is an illustrator who recently moved shop from Chicago, USA to Melbourne, Australia and has fallen madly in love with koalas. She paints because it relaxes her and makes her feel a little less crazy than usual.

DONNA SMITH

Donna Smith lives with her husband and three children in Victoria. Donna loves everything about books and literature. She has had several poems and children's stories published in journals and anthologies. Donna won the 2008 Billabong Valley Writing Competition (preschool section) and is enjoying study: a Bachelor of Arts focused on Writing and Literature.

SHAUN TAN

Shaun Tan grew up in the northern suburbs of Perth, Western Australia. In school he became known as the 'good drawer' which partly compensated for always being the shortest kid in every class. His books, including *The Rabbits*, *The Red Tree*, *The Lost Thing* and the acclaimed wordless novel *The Arrival*, have been widely translated throughout Europe, Asia and South America, and enjoyed by readers of all ages.

DIANNE TOUCHELL

Dianne Touchell is a bookseller from Perth who loves the smell of new books. She has had a life-long fear of Santa Claus, the Easter Bunny, the Tooth Fairy and any other large uninvited guest who sneaks into the house in the middle of the night. She is also wary of bean bags following an unfortunate incident involving her being stuck in one for five hours.

ANGELA VERNON

Angela Vernon has been writing for almost as long as she can remember (quite a long time). She loves anything spooky, magical or mythical and especially enjoys telling scary stories to children! But only if they promise to sleep with their night-lights on.

GABRIELLE WANG

An award-winning author and illustrator of books for children and young adults, Gabrielle loves writing stories with a touch of horror and fantasy. When she's not writing she likes to read, travel and go horseback riding.

STEPHEN WHITESIDE

Stephen Whiteside has been writing rhyming verse for adults and children for many years. Many of his poems have been published in magazines or anthologies (both in Australia and overseas), or won awards. He has also self-published four collections of his poems, and been nominated for several Bush Laureate Awards. Stephen's poems are written to be recited, and he performs frequently at folk festivals. He works as a medical practitioner (GP) in an outer Melbourne suburb.

CAROLE WILKINSON

Carole is the award-winning author of the *Dragonkeeper* trilogy, as well as many other books for children. She is a meticulous researcher who finds it difficult to stop reading and begin writing. Carole is married, has a daughter and lives in inner-city Melbourne.

LILI WILKINSON

Lili is a reader and writer of Young Adult fiction. She manages insideadog.com.au, the Centre for Youth Literature's website for teenagers, and is the author of *Joan of Arc: the story of Jehanne Darc*, *Scatterheart* and *Angel Fish*.

ALISTAIR WOOD

Alistair has been drawing since he was two-years-old. He is a fan of writer Edgar Allan Poe, actor Vincent Price and director Tim Burton. He wrote and illustrated this poem when he was nine-years-old. He is now in Year 5 and wants to be an animator when he grows up.

ROBYNE YOUNG

Robyne wrote her first poem about mermaids in Grade 3 — not a scary subject at all — and has written only a few poems since. She has worked as a journalist, copywriter, events manager and lecturer, but loves to write fiction and has had a number of short stories published, as well as contributing to the progressive illustrated novel *Murray Time* set around her home city of Albury–Wodonga after the 2003 bushfires.

Her most challenging writing assignment has been to create sixty words for the side of a birdseed packet. Perhaps her first "tweet"?

If you'd like the short without the scary,
you need to read

short

a collection of
interesting short stories
and other stuff from
some surprising and intelligent people

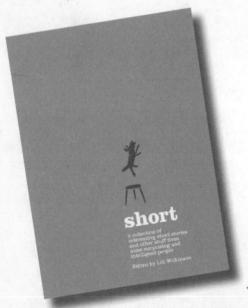

short

a collection of
interesting short stories
and other stuff from
some surprising and
intelligent people

Edited by Lili Wilkinson

edited by Lili Wilkinson